DAVID WARD

AMULET BOOKS
NEW YORK

ACKNOWLEDGMENTS

My thanks to my editor Maggie Lehrman for making this a better story, and to my agent Scott Treimel who understands so well the journey of every book.

Library of Congress Cataloging-in-Publication Data

Ward, David, 1967–
Between two ends / by David Ward.
p. cm.
Summary: Trying to help his father deal with his longstanding depression, Yeats and his parents visit his grandmother's old and eerie house, where he discovers a pair of pirate bookends that unlock a thirty-year-old secret that Yeats must try to resolve by entering the exotic world of *The Arabian Nights*.
ISBN 978-0-8109-9714-1 (alk. paper)
[1. Books and reading—Fiction. 2. Characters in literature—Fiction. 3. Pirates—Fiction. 4. Adventure and adventurers—Fiction. 5. Arabian nights—Fiction.] I. Title.
PZ7.W1873En 2011
[Fic]—dc22
2010023696

Printed and bound in U.S.A.
10 9 8 7 6 5 4 3 2 1

Amulet Books are available at special discounts when purchased in quantity for premiums and promotions as well as fundraising or educational use. Special editions can also be created to specification. For details, contact specialmarkets@abramsbooks.com or the address below.

THE ART OF BOOKS SINCE 1949
115 West 18th Street
New York, NY 10011
www.abramsbooks.com

For my sisters, Colleen and Sharon.
May this story bring back fond memories and
perhaps a little of the magic of Gran's house.

CONTENTS

PROLOGUE

Dust rose in stifling clouds into the Arabian sky. Struggling frantically to reach his companion, the boy shouted, "I won't let them take you!" The girl stared, confused, standing in between the black-robed men who held her. Her wide brown eyes shifted feverishly. Fruit sellers and villagers at the nearest stalls stopped their business to watch the drama unfold.

Breaking free from his captors, the boy lunged, but he was knocked to the ground before he could reach the girl. "Listen to me!" he pleaded. "You're bewitched. We don't belong here."

The girl tugged at her long black curls. She made to kneel, to reach out to the boy, but strong

hands kept her on her feet. The boy's fair hair and pale complexion contrasted sharply with the people in the market, but she couldn't remember why that was important. Hardly distinguishable from the overwhelming odor of cattle dung and fruit, a spicy, pungent smell hung in the air. The girl's heart raced with excitement now at the wonders around her. Her feet wanted to dance. Wherever the black-robed men wanted to take her, she felt no danger in going with them. After all, they knew her name.

"Please," she murmured. "Do not harm him."

"My lady Shaharazad," said a tall man beside her. "Your father will be mad with worry. How you left the garden without escort is beyond my knowledge." He cast a dark glance at his men. "Take the lady back to the palace. At once!" The black-robed men forced a path through the throngs of people, opening the way to a grand palace in the distance.

The girl's eyes grew wider at the splendor of the whitewashed fortress with its golden turrets. The boy shook his head to clear the fog spreading over his mind. "We've got to get back to the library," he stammered sluggishly.

A powerful foot pinned the boy to the dust. Uttering a final plea he shouted, "Shari! Please! Let's go home!"

Before the girl could answer, the men closed around her and she disappeared in a mass of swirling black robes and glinting scimitars. The tall man turned back. He waited for the crowd to envelop the girl and her guards. Then, hands on his hips, he regarded the boy with forbidding eyes. Tapping his sword, he ordered the remaining guards, "Chop off his head!"

1

A HOUSE OF
DEAD POETS

The gate was shut. Patchwork shadows shifted over untended grounds and broken masonry. From the gloom of overhanging trees a tired mansion stared at Yeats through shuttered windows. All through the winding roads of "Poet's Lane" he envisioned something more glorious—medieval, perhaps, a place displaying a coat of arms or ceremonial swords above the door. After all, his grandparents had come from England a long time ago and must have brought some curious old country things with them. He glanced back at the road that had brought them to this place and then to his parents, who sat motionless in the car.

For much of the ride his mother had been strangely silent, watching the brick houses and weeping willows blur by. Her malaise seemed to deepen as she glanced from her husband's white-knuckled grip on the steering wheel to the street signs. Tennyson, Swift, Coleridge: every street named for dead poets.

Yeats's father, Dr. William Trafford, quoted each poet as they drove, mumbling snippets of ballads and sonnets as if offering ride-along eulogies. Propping up his glasses for the fifth time in several minutes, he gave a nervous cough. When he brought the car to a halt, Mrs. Trafford gave a long sigh. She winced when Yeats leapt out of the car.

Yeats toyed with the latch on the gate. A cobbled path meandered through weeping willows to darkness and the front door. *Sinister* would have held promise, but this house appeared . . . *forgotten*.

"Does anyone even live here?" he murmured.

His father smiled feebly. Leaning out the window, he called, "Heads up, son! It's an interesting place. At least, it was when I was growing up. There's lots to do." He cast a nervous glance at the yard, then turned to his wife. "Right, Faith?"

"No, William," she said. "Which is precisely why we're only staying the night. It's a house of dead poets."

"I'll be fine," Yeats interjected. "And don't worry, Mom." He swung back to the car. "I'll get the bags, then, Dad?"

"Thanks, son. That would be nice."

As Yeats hurried past the open car window to the trunk he noticed his father furiously polishing his glasses.

William blew on the lenses before submitting them to another round of nervous cleaning with his handkerchief. This was a "revitalization weekend," another attempt at curing his bouts of depression, and likely, the last with his wife accompanying him. The tension was unbearable.

The university where they lived was quiet in the final month of summer, leaving him free from academic responsibilities until the fall term. But most revitalization weekends were spent at a spa or the hot springs and not on a long drive into the country. It did not help that the weather was turning foul. William pursed his lips. What could he do? This is where it all had happened. He cleared his throat. "I told Mum we'd stay for the weekend."

Silence.

Yeats froze with his hand on the half-open trunk. His mother's profile stiffened. "You never said that. You said 'for the day.'"

Yeats swallowed. This was it, the last straw. He looked down the length of the car and then said loudly, "Mom, I'll take your bags too." When she didn't respond he closed the trunk and listened.

"Come on, Faith," his father was saying. "We're here now. We can decide later. These things take time. There are no guarantees. I can't predict what will happen or if anything happens at all. It's been twenty years!"

Through the rear window Yeats watched them exchange glances. He breathed again when his mother, barely audible, said, "I know. It's this place. It makes me uneasy."

"It never used to make you uneasy."

"I didn't know much back then. Still don't."

The door of the house opened with a creak. Someone stepped onto the porch, but branches blocked Yeats from seeing the figure clearly.

His mother leaned out of the passenger door, hooking Yeats with a glare. "Don't tell her how long we're staying in case our plans change. Don't mention what we think of your school. Say 'Everything is fine.' You can call her whatever you want. She won't tell you, so you'll have to decide on something."

"Call her Gran," his father said.

Gran. He barely remembered her. She had an English accent. She had visited them one Christmas, long ago. And yet, through a thousand kitchen conversations with his parents, Yeats knew her thoughts on every topic. His parents were moving now, unbuckling seat belts and opening doors.

The instructions continued.

"Avoid the subject of religion."

"Oh, Faith!" William groaned. There was an intake of breath. "Here she comes," William said.

His body had gone rigid. "Get out of the car. She's on the stairs."

"Whatever happens . . . Yeats! Look at me!" His mother got out, her eyes wide. "This is an odd place. Stay away from closed doors, all right?"

Yeats frowned.

The car doors slammed simultaneously.

Inside the house, the vibration reached to the farthest room. One book teetered on its shelf and collapsed, creating an enormous cloud of dust. The dust spread, reaching the main window. The particles splashed against the pane as if eager to see the new arrivals.

Yeats's mother rallied her confidence. "Hold my hand," she said to Yeats.

"Mom. I'm twelve."

"*I* need your hand."

Now not only was his throat constricting but Yeats's spine prickled as well. He watched his father head up the path toward the house. "Maybe we shouldn't stay," he suggested, setting down the luggage. "This doesn't feel right. Dad's really nervous. And you're jumpy! Let's go home."

And *home* meant keeping the specters away from his father for a little longer. Depression usually followed a revitalization weekend—plunging his father further into gloom instead of bringing him out of it. If he could keep his mother hoping, keep things normal, their little family might stay together.

She shook her head. "Your father has to do this. At least, he says he does. And why we need to stay the weekend . . ." She tucked several blond strands behind his ear. "Don't be angry, Yeats."

"I'm not."

"You're scowling," she countered.

He shrugged. "It's just frustrating."

She patted his cheek. "I know. And you're a hero. You bear his burden as if it were your own. You're as loyal as a badger." Her eyes flickered to the house. "But I won't let this go on much longer."

Yeats wiped the scowl from his face. "There. Now, please tell me why everyone is so nervous about this place."

Her hand trembled. "It's not just the place. It's an anniversary of sorts. A twentieth. Come on,

Son. Come and meet your grandmother. And her house!"

Ahead of them Yeats saw his father embrace Gran.

"Faith!" croaked a voice.

"Hello, Mum."

Yeats saw tangled white hair, a robe—not a dress. Unlike with his father there was no distant sadness about her. Rather, it seemed to Yeats that she took in her long-absent family with wise, experienced eyes. Breaking from her daughter-in-law's embrace, she looked at Yeats.

"Oh, don't worry, young man. I won't kiss you. I'm not so old as to forget unwanted affection."

Despite his apprehension he broke into a grin. Her confidence was contagious and a welcome relief from his father's anxious banter throughout the car ride.

She returned the smile. "'Drink to me only with thine eyes, and I will pledge with mine.'" She raised her hand, toasting him. "That was Ben Jonson. But you knew that."

"We haven't pushed poetry," his mother said.

Gran winked at Yeats. "It's never too late to become a poet. My goodness, you're a strapping lad!" She held out her arms. Her grip was sure and firm. Yeats patted her back clumsily, hoping she wouldn't comment on his long hair.

"I haven't been squeezed by so handsome a young man in a thousand years!" She took his hands. "Goodness! Look at those paws. The size comes from your side, Faith. We never had much height." She beckoned. "Inside. The tea is fresh."

Old stones peeked out from the wildness of the garden as they mounted the steps. "What did that used to be?" Yeats murmured. The remains of a wall and a fountain's gaping mouth watched him take the last stair.

The kitchen was wide and bright and the kettle heralded their entry with a burst of whistling steam. There were bundles of dried plants hanging from the ceiling and the scents of the garden lingered when the door closed. Several doorways branched to hallways that hinted at the mansion's deceptive nature: the house was secretly enormous.

Around a short wall the kitchen opened to a dining room and beyond that . . . Yeats caught his mother's gaze arrested by a door at the back.

A cat scuttled across his feet.

"Odysseus!" Gran called. She scooped up the cat and scratched under his chin. Then she turned to Yeats and handed him the cat. "He owns the place. At least, he believes so. Half the time I do too. Would you take charge of him? I will be busy. He dines twice a day—one treat before bed—and needs to be let out for personal reasons as requested."

Odysseus placed his forelegs firmly against Yeats's chest and gave him a long green-eyed stare. As Yeats turned, Odysseus swatted playfully at his hair.

"You like that, do you?" Yeats asked.

"Ah," Gran said. "You will be good friends."

William stood paralyzed, transfixed by the cat.

"Yes." Gran smiled. "Odysseus is still with us."

"Mum," William said. "He can't be—it's impossible . . ."

"There are stranger things than Odysseus in this house, my dear. You should know that."

A bell jingled somewhere. "Ah, Mr. Sutcliff," Gran said, snapping her fingers.

"Sutcliff?" William blanched even whiter.

Faith frowned. "He's here, Mum? He lives *here*?"

There was a long pause while Gran reached for a box of tea. "Of course he lives *here*. Upstairs. In William's old room."

William wiped his glistening forehead. Whoever Mr. Sutcliff was, Yeats decided not to like him. They had been in the house hardly five minutes and twice Yeats had seen his father upset. He squared his shoulders and prepared for the worst. His mother looked ready to walk out the door.

Gran fussed at the stove and returned with a tray of tea and cookies. "Would you prefer him on the streets, William? Hungry, lost, *alone*."

William squeezed his eyes shut. "Of course not. But perhaps we should go."

Yeats locked eyes with his mother.

"Where, William?" Gran asked quietly. "Where will you go this time?"

Yeats pressed his cheek against Odysseus.

"Don't worry, little guy," he whispered half to the cat and half to himself.

William sat down heavily. "We've had this conversation before."

"Since before Yeats was born," Gran agreed.

"I'd like to leave Yeats out of it," Faith said.

"Why?"

"Because he's doing so well. Good in school, sports, and for the first time in his life, he's spending more time with friends than worrying about his father."

William shifted uncomfortably.

Yeats winced. It was true. He had been going out more lately, but it was difficult to call anyone a *friend*, as yet. He'd met a few interesting kids on the university endowment lands, but he didn't want to raise too much hope. His family always moved before anything could stick—they had lived all over the United States. He looked around the room. "Can someone tell me what is going on?"

No one said anything.

He maneuvered Odysseus onto his shoulder. "I

know something happened here. A long time ago. Something bad. I want to help."

"You see?" Faith threw up her arms. "Just when we're getting him to a normal space, something comes up."

"How did you know something happened *here*?" his father asked sharply.

Yeats touched noses with the cat. "You and Mom talk at night. At least, you used to."

"Handsome *and* intelligent." Gran nodded approvingly.

The bell jingled again.

"Yeats." Gran pushed the tray forward. "Will you take these to Mr. Sutcliff, please? Odysseus will show you the way."

On cue, the cat broke free from Yeats's arms and leapt to the floor. His eyes held Yeats's momentarily before he padded for the stairs. William drew his legs back as if the cat were poison.

Yeats stared down the hallway. Taking tea to someone he had never met, someone who rang a bell for service, was a little weird. His father began polishing his glasses again. His mother looked furious.

Yeats reached for the tray. "Love to."

Gran didn't let go. Her grip was strong, as powerful as her smile. "Mr. Sutcliff will eat two of the cookies. Don't eat the remaining two. I will collect those tonight when I take him dinner. Later you may have as many as you like."

"Why doesn't he eat all of them?"

Her gaze flickered to his parents. "He is waiting for someone."

Odysseus yowled.

"My, my, Yeats." Gran shook her head. "Flaxen hair! And just look at those eyes. They're William's! Insatiable curiosity. That will lead to adventure. Off you go! The tea is growing cold."

2

THE
WISHING WELL

Outside in the garden and high up in the tallest tree, a crow bobbed on an evergreen branch. The bird spotted a grub clinging to an enormous pinecone. The crow pecked at the cone and set it spinning on its slender stem. After a second round of pecking the grub fell and landed on the ledge of a short wall far below.

The ledge formed the lip of an old well long overgrown by vines and branches. The crow cocked its head and began to shift from foot to foot, weighing what to do next. When the grub squirmed tantalizingly from the ledge, the crow made up its mind. It flew down with a raucous cry and landed on the well top.

Just as it stretched out its beak to snatch the grub, a blast of cold air suddenly shot up from the well mouth and set the crow's feathers blowing. The bird flinched and waited for the wind to stop. Several seconds passed and the wind suddenly blew itself out like a breath. There was a pause, and then, from the deepest depths, there came a low moan. The lament echoed ominously and rose upward, vibrating and shaking the foundations of the well.

The crow froze. It cocked its head first one way, then turned the other way to listen. When the next blast struck, the crow flinched and prepared to fly. The grub was bounced by the shaking stones to the edge of the well mouth and then hurled skyward the moment it hit the wind. Just as the crow made to follow, the moan transformed into an unearthly intake of breath. The wind changed direction and fled down the well.

The crow felt the pull immediately and found itself caught in the grip of a vortex at the center of the well mouth. The bird flapped its wings with all its strength. Its tail stuck out earthward, straight as a poker, as if some unseen hand had taken hold of it.

The crow began to tire. In another moment its wings would cease to beat and it would be sucked down into darkness and to calamity. With Herculean effort the crow leaned to one side and found the wind not quite so strong as in the center. It leaned farther still and found a last burst of energy. With a final stroke the crow pulled free of the well and shot out into the brightness and safety of the garden. The ground trembled and then fell still. The moaning turned to an unhappy murmur and finally died away.

High up on a branch the crow preened itself soothingly. It hunted no more grubs for the rest of the day and settled down for a nap to sleep off the recent horror. The garden fell quiet.

Near the well was a set of tiles leading up to the remains of a fountain. Water had long since stopped flowing and all that could be seen of the basin was a single corner, peeking out from a thicket of grass. The earth around the tiles was loose and cracked. One of the tiles was broken and dislodged from the others and shook from time to time, as if something was pushing up against it from below.

There was a scraping sound, like a metal tool working against pottery. Soon, there came a series of chipping noises, like a pickax attacking a ceramic surface. From time to time the well would shake and moan and the sounds beneath the tile would stop. As soon as the moaning ended the scraping and chipping would begin again.

High in the tree the crow raised a wary eye from beneath its wing. The tile began to rock a little on its edge. Seconds later an object—sharp, metallic, and no longer than a sewing needle— burst through a growing crack in the tile and into the garden light. It was a sword.

3

MR. SUTCLIFF

Yeats made for the hall. The fresh scent of the kitchen gave way to the odor of old books, leather, and mothballs. While the outside of the house appeared to be rotting, the inside was full of treasures. Brightly painted tribal masks stared at him as he passed through a sitting room, while opposite them, knights grimaced from a floor-to-ceiling painting. There were carvings and colored stones on every table. The floor creaked beneath his feet and he wondered if he should have removed his shoes. No one had said anything about that.

Odysseus waited at the bottom stair. A stained glass window provided kaleidoscopic illumination to the yawning darkness above. It was a narrow

passage, each step worn by countless footfalls. Natural light caught the edge of the top. Odysseus padded up.

The first stair creaked horribly. Yeats cringed and a drop of tea splashed his leg. Still warm. His steps turned into a cacophony of squeaks and squawks. "Come on, Yeats!" he scolded himself. He took a deep breath and scowled.

A resounding silence followed the last squawk at the top of the stairs and the air stopped moving. It felt as if the room had been closed for many years. An old man sat near the window with Odysseus at his feet. His hair was whiter than Gran's and came down past his shoulders. He stirred and his eyes widened.

"William!" he exclaimed. His knuckles whitened on the chair arm. "I knew it! I knew you would come back. Good boy! And where is Shaharazad? Is my granddaughter with you?"

"I'm Yeats."

"Yeats?" Mr. Sutcliff stood stiffly. He searched Yeats's face, his disappointment obvious. "No, you're not Yeats. I did think at one time that you should have been Auden or Milton. But your grandmother told me to mind my own poets. Your father, now *he* was Yeats."

"That was my grandfather," Yeats said. "Yeats William Trafford."

The old man regarded the cat. Odysseus rubbed against his legs. Mr. Sutcliff sighed and leaned down to scratch the animal's ears again. Then he did something even more alarming.

"Is he there, Odysseus?" he asked. "Is there a boy standing, holding my tea? Or have I imagined him?"

For an answer, Odysseus trotted over and rolled his tail along Yeats's legs. Mr. Sutcliff nodded. He sighed again, reached into his pocket, and pulled out a pair of spectacles. He smoothed the front of his shirt and straightened his back. "I see. So, you are Yeats and you look the spitting image of William. Well, come here, boy!"

Startled, Yeats stumbled forward, spilling more tea down his leg. He desperately wanted his arms free for protection, but they were holding the tray. The old man stood, peering into his face. Mr.

Sutcliff suddenly reached out and took his chin and Yeats stifled a gasp. His grip was as sure as Gran's. His eyebrows were horrifically bushy.

"Hmmm," he murmured. "Intelligent. Curious. Reliable." He shifted Yeats's chin to look at his profile. "Burgeoning courage as well."

Yeats turned his head aside. "I brought your tea," he said. Mr. Sutcliff did not seem to notice. Instead, he tapped his lips thoughtfully with his fingers. Yeats considered laying the tea and cookies on the floor and bolting for the stairs. He had met many quirky people at the university, but Mr. Sutcliff was rapidly rising to the top of the list.

"Is William downstairs?"

"Yes."

"And he is a man?"

Yeats lowered the tea to the floor. "He is my father."

The old man grunted. "I see. And your mother?"

"Her name is Faith."

"Faith?" Mr. Sutcliff felt for a pipe on the table without releasing Yeats from his gaze. "Now there's a good name. Plain, mind you, but solid—versatile, even. The stuff of all good poetry. Yes, indeed!" His last words were muffled as his lips took the pipe. Yeats waited for him to light it, but Mr. Sutcliff merely sucked the end comfortably. "'Now these three remain: faith, hope and love. But the greatest of these is love.'" He returned to his window. "I believe in that. I really do."

Yeats gritted his teeth. Gran wanted the tea delivered and Yeats was determined to see it through. "Would you like your tea, sir?"

The old man motioned with his pipe. Yeats took a few hesitant steps, then hastily set down the tray. He returned to the door. He needed to get downstairs and make sure his parents weren't fighting.

"William . . . *is a man*," Mr. Sutcliff murmured. He shook his head. After an uncomfortable silence he added, "Will he see me?"

"I don't know, sir," Yeats answered. "I imagine he would."

"Imagine?" The old man spun quickly.

Yeats readied himself against the door frame.

Mr. Sutcliff brushed long strands of hair from his eyes. "Yes, *imagine*. That's the key. Has he the courage, I wonder?" He tapped the pipe against his lips. "I don't even know if it's possible. We don't know enough, do we? Perhaps . . . perhaps with enough *sincerity* it might . . . I don't know." He was silent for so long, Yeats thought Mr. Sutcliff had forgotten him. Then the old man tapped his temple with an idea and spryly spun around. "Can *you*? Can you, Yeats? Dare you, I wonder? Would *you* have enough courage?"

"I've got to go now," Yeats stammered.

Mr. Sutcliff pointed his pipe. "Remember the words, my boy? Do you remember?" The old man closed his eyes:

"'Come away, O human child!

To the waters and the wild

With a faery, hand in hand,

For the world's more full of weeping than you can
  understand.'

"That was William Butler Yeats—your name-sake. But I'm sure you knew that."

Yeats fled, landing on the stairs two at a time

and making such a commotion he expected them to break at any moment. He slowed near the kitchen only to find Odysseus trotting alongside him. The cat glared disapprovingly.

Yeats gasped. "Don't look at me like that!" When he realized his hands were shaking he turned them into fists. He glanced back at the stairs, then stepped into the adult conversation.

His parents were sipping tea. He was comforted to see them sitting next to each other and his father's glasses back on his nose. Odysseus demanded to be picked up.

"How did that go?" Gran asked.

Yeats couldn't tell if she was speaking to him or to the cat.

"I gave him his tea," he said.

"Good lad." Gran put the cat down. "You must be more careful on those stairs, dear. They aren't used to such youthful energy. My goodness, you sounded like an Oliphant in distress."

Still panting, Yeats stammered, "He thought I was someone else. He thought I knew his granddaughter. Shaharazad or something?"

His father's cup rattled violently, followed swiftly by a curse as the tea shot over his knees. His mother's teeth were clenched and the blood drained from her face. His father looked as if he was going to faint.

4

SHAHARAZAD
(SHAH-HAH-RAH-ZAHD)

Gran rested her hands on Yeats's shoulders. Her words, however, were directed at his parents. "You are being silly—both of you. He is her grandfather, after all. And it is high time we all heard that name again." She stopped Faith's protest. "I know what you are thinking. I understand your fear."

William rose slowly. "Mum, I came here to fix *me*. This has nothing to do with Yeats."

"How do you know that?"

"Because he wasn't there!"

Yeats appealed to Gran. "I wasn't *where*?"

She squeezed his shoulders. "Patience." She

looked at William. "He needs to know. Look at him! If anyone can help, it is this boy."

"Mum . . . ," William protested. "We've just stepped in the door."

"And the name that has pierced your heart for twenty years, William . . . twenty years, has surfaced in that time. You, my son, like Frodo, were wounded indefinitely—in dark circumstances. And you have endured the hurt beyond merit. But now, the time for healing has come."

"Mom?" Yeats whispered.

His mother faced his father. "She's right. Everything she said is right. No more running, William. I am tired. This is it. Do something or changes are coming. I mean it."

Yeats silently cursed himself. Why couldn't he have kept his mouth shut about the girl? Mr. Sutcliff was obviously crazy. If only he hadn't taken the tea to him. Now his mother was ready for a divorce if his father didn't change.

William glanced furtively past the kitchen to the back room. The house had grown peculiarly quiet. The clock ticked loudly, its pendulum swinging like

the indecision written on his face. Finally he lifted
his chin. He looked at Gran, then at his wife. "All
right." Yeats looked up hopefully.

In the garden, there was a loud cracking sound.
The echo reached the house. Faith sat bolt upright.
"What was *that?*"

Gran shrugged and then motioned to the dining
room table. "It's an old place, Faith, with many
sounds. I tune them out most days. Most likely it's
the well. It was broken many years ago. Lord knows
how many old wishes are still rattling around and
trying to get out. More cookies and tea?"

"I remember that well," William said miserably.
"It certainly never granted my wish."

They moved to the table in uncomfortable
silence.

After refilling the teapot Gran tapped her lap
for Odysseus. Yeats regarded his father. Only
twenty-four hours ago Yeats had been pleasantly
contemplating the eternal month of August. And
then his father had sprung a surprise trip, "for a
day or two," a car ride to the country. He knew
something was wrong; his parents were arguing

over something. But the summer sun and the hope of new friends had soothed his worries.

Gran sipped her tea.

Faith patted her son's hand. "Don't worry."

"About *what*?"

"Just don't worry. And stop scowling."

Gran said to Yeats, "You like stories, don't you?"

He nodded.

"Then I will tell you two stories, for they are very closely attached. Make yourself comfortable."

Yeats settled in his chair. He was used to stories.

"A long time ago, in ancient Arabia, India, China, and Persia, stories were told and written down. They have been told and retold over the centuries and no one is certain of their original versions, much like Grimms' fairy tales. Some of them you have heard before: Aladdin and his lamp? Perhaps even Ali Baba and the Forty Thieves, or Sinbad? You have? Good."

She continued. "But what many children of today do not know is that some of the stories are linked by one: the story of Shaharazad and One Thousand and One Arabian Nights."

William groaned.

Gran said, "Shaharazad was the daughter of the royal adviser, or vizier, to the King. She was both courageous and beautiful—blessed with the extraordinary gift of insight like her father. Her wisdom, however, came into question one day when she put herself in mortal danger to save her people."

Yeats reached for a cookie.

"The King was happy, living in love and wealth. Then one day he was betrayed by his wife and his brother. A terrible madness seized him. Furious, he gripped a spear and hurled it at his brother. The blade missed its target and drove into the heart of his wife. Stricken with grief and anger, the King banished his brother. In the days to come nothing could ease the King's pain. By law he was required to marry again or abdicate the throne. But his heart could not find the courage to trust anyone again."

"What did he do?" Yeats asked.

"He devised a spiteful plan. A dreadful plan. He decided that he would marry again, according to the laws of the land, but that this time he would kill his bride on their wedding night."

"Not exactly fair, is it?" Yeats said. "And how would that keep him married? If he killed her, he wouldn't be married anymore."

"Right you are. But if the King took a different girl each night . . ."

"He killed one *each night?*"

Gran nodded. "He did. When Shaharazad heard of this she immediately offered to be the King's bride."

"So, she was crazy as well as beautiful?"

Faith rested her face in her hands. "Shhh. Listen, Yeats."

"Oh, she wasn't crazy," Gran assured him. "She had a plan. Her father tried to dissuade her. As the royal vizier he knew the volatile condition of the King better than anyone. But his daughter was persuasive. It wasn't long before she married the King."

"And he killed her?" Yeats asked.

"On the wedding night, the King told Shaharazad that it was time for her to die. But, wise girl that she was, she answered, 'Come, my lord, you are tired and ill at ease. Let me tell you a story to calm your mind.' The King did not know what to do with this proposal, so he answered, 'If your story allows me to sleep peacefully without the nightmares that plague me, I will let you live another day.' And it did. For the girl had studied the poets and stories of many countries and could tell a tale like no one else. Story after story she told, night after night, calming the King, until a thousand and one nights had passed."

Odysseus purred loudly.

"Then what happened?"

"Ah," said Gran. "The King dealt with his brother, through battle, and he finally gave his trust to his queen. The story ends with Shaharazad telling the King's story to their own children."

"So she lived?" Yeats asked.

"She did. And she became an Eastern heroine of the highest standing."

Yeats thought again of the old man upstairs. "What does all that have to do with Dad?"

William cleared his throat. His eyes shifted

again to the back room. "Over twenty years ago," he began, "when I was your age, a girl came to live with us. Her parents had died a year or two before in a car accident, and her grandfather, Mr. Sutcliff, asked if she could stay."

Gran said, "I've known the Sutcliffs all my life. I couldn't turn them down."

"Her name . . . ," William continued, ". . . was Shaharazad."

"Shaharazad," Yeats whispered.

"Indeed. Though we all called her Shari. That's her there." He nodded to a picture.

A shapely face, white teeth, long black hair. Her eyes challenged.

"She's pretty," Yeats said.

"Yes," his father murmured. "I never noticed. We were too busy having adventures. Her mother was Persian." Yeats nodded and continued to look at the photograph. The girl had dusky skin and sculpted eyebrows. Her hands, resting on her lap, were both delicate and clever.

"And she was well named," Gran added. "Just like Shaharazad she lived with tragedy around her. And yet she hunted for ways to help the family through troubled times. A Persian princess." She sighed. "She was entranced by the story of the Arabian Nights. She so wanted to turn a sad story into a happy one."

William unclenched his fists. "Shari and I became good friends. This house and the land around it were our playground. The creek, the woods . . ."

"The library," Gran interrupted.

"Everywhere," William hurried on. "Shari was wild—*adventurous* isn't even the right word— *fearless* is better. She wanted to save the world. She combed these woods looking for things to save. We rescued a kitten from a rotten tree, mice that had lost their mother, anything that breathed and needed saving." He suddenly stopped speaking and loosened his shirt collar. He removed a necklace crafted of worn leather. Two objects hung in the middle: a clear marble with a hole through its middle and a tiny silver bell. It gave a faint tinkle as he laid it in Yeats's hand.

For as long as he could remember, his father

had worn the necklace regardless of whether he was dressed formally or casually. When Yeats was a toddler he would play with the necklace until asked to give it back. It was always a treat to be allowed to hold it.

His father pressed the marble and bell into Yeats's hand. For the briefest moment, the other people in the room faded. His father spoke with clarity and certainty.

"There," he said. "That's better. I believe with all my heart that you will be safer with that in your possession. Don't lose it."

"I won't," Yeats answered. "Thanks, Dad."

"Well, that's a first," said Faith. "That's been your good-luck charm for as long we've been married. Never thought I'd see the day."

"I remember the bell," said Gran. "It was Shari's."

Yeats slipped the necklace around his neck. The marble was cool against his skin. He felt a little embarrassed by all the attention.

"Yes, it was," his father murmured. The thought returned him to the story. "One day, Shari and I were in the back room. Mum—your gran—was out. We were reading some of the books in the library. . . ."

"*One* of the books," Gran corrected.

"One of the books—the *Arabian Nights*. There were several versions in the library and Shari insisted that we read them all. Something strange happened then, although what it was, I don't exactly remember."

"What do you mean?" Yeats asked.

His father stood up. "Have you got any beer, Mum?"

"No."

"Wine?"

"There's a flask of Scotch on the second shelf to your left. I keep it for Mr. Sutcliff's nightcaps. Don't spill, please. Odysseus likes it too."

Yeats toyed with the necklace at his throat. He had never seen his father drink before. His mother said nothing but was clearly agitated. One more nail in the coffin, Yeats thought. He had to do something, but he was trapped in this room.

William sat down again, this time with a shot

glass. He shuddered as he drained the golden liquid. "Shari was taken away," he gasped.

"While reading Collfield's unexpurgated version of the *Arabian Nights*," Gran interrupted. "Why do you keep avoiding the facts?"

William's eyes had glazed over. "They took Shari." He looked at his son. "It nearly brought me over the edge. I can hardly remember anything. It sent Mr. Sutcliff mad."

Gran swirled her tea wrathfully. "He's not mad. That's the easy way out. This was not an everyday occurrence! Her abductors came from a special place. You know what I mean."

William stammered, "I had to return, Yeats, to see where it all happened, for the hope of closure."

There was a long pause.

Faith's frown turned into an astonished "oh." "You've always said this story was a dream. I assumed what really happened was buried underneath your grief. What are you trying to say, William?"

Gran fidgeted. "That's all, William? That's all you're going to say?"

"For now."

"May I add to it?"

"Not yet, Mum. Please, we haven't been here an hour."

Odysseus stretched luxuriously.

"Do you think, William," Gran said, and peered at him sagely, "that more time will ease the facts? While time may be a healer, inaction most definitely *is not*. Your story leaves unsatisfying, gaping holes."

William turned to Yeats, and father and son regarded each other.

"I don't need to know," Yeats assured him, "unless it helps."

"I'll start by talking to Mr. Sutcliff," his father said. "That's as good a place as any."

Gran raised her eyebrows. "Everything starts with a story, my boy. Even poems. I thought you could start at the beginning."

"That's why I'll go to Mr. Sutcliff, Mum."

Gran shook her head. "You and a missing girl are the beginning. I've lived my life without knowing the secrets of this house. At least, not all of them.

We must start with what you can remember. And that may take some digging!"

"What secrets?" Yeats asked. His skin prickled.

Patting the wall, Gran said, "This home has an extraordinary history, my boy."

"Don't, Mum," William pleaded.

"Why not? It is Yeats's history too. Besides, I promised him two stories. And now, for the second tale, and one that is closer to his heart than he knows." She ran her finger lovingly along the oak window ledge. "Your great-great-grandfather Philip Walter Trafford was a collector of sorts. His antiques were rather unusual."

"How?" Yeats asked.

"Well, they were . . ." She waved her hand, fishing for the right word. "Ancient. Connected to literature in some way and . . ."

"Yes?" Yeats encouraged.

Gran leaned forward. "Magical."

Yeats raised his eyebrows.

His mother snorted. "If it wasn't so absurd I might be amused. Doesn't sound very scientific."

"And so you have been brought up to believe,"

Gran said. "Science is so limiting when it is the only lens you use." Before Faith could reply, Gran added, "Grandpa Trafford did not share your faith in science. Oh, he loved chemistry and the apothecary arts to be sure. But he also understood their source."

"What do you mean?" said Yeats after an uncomfortable silence.

"Good!" Gran tapped Yeats's hand. "That is proper science. Clarify the terms so that we can understand one another better. Magic is what we are talking about. Not the silly kind found at a country fair with tricks and gimmicks. No— your great-great-grandfather was interested in something deeper. Something so grand the ancients could only express it through anthro-pomorphism, gods and goddesses, through Muses and inspiration."

Gran indicated the room with the closed door. "There are some very old books in the library, from a time when people did not rely on science as they do these days." She nodded knowingly. "Grandfather Trafford loved the great books of literature. He said they were the best reminders of the first and greatest act of inspiration."

"And what was that?" asked Yeats.

Gran raised her eyebrow. "Creation."

Yeats looked from one adult to another. His father's face was drawn tightly, not with skepticism but with concern. His mother looked at the floor, smirking. Gran stared back at him unblinkingly.

"Oh," said Yeats.

Gran continued. "Your great-great-grandfather collected as many of the greatest works as he could. Paintings, sculptures, antiques of all kinds, even a pair of bookends made by a Dutch sculptor."

"Bookends," William repeated. "I remember those."

"Mr. Sutcliff believes the bookends are the key," Gran said. "Which is why I mentioned them."

Yeats gaped at his father, then at Gran. His mother spoke for him.

"You're not serious? I know the house is weird, but please!" She appealed to William. "You said that you and Shari had wild imaginations, that perhaps . . ." She checked herself when she saw her son's face. "Yeats? Would you go outside for a few minutes? Apparently I've been excluded from some important conversations." She glared at his father. "I want some clarity before we go any further. Perhaps Yeats could take Odysseus for a stroll?"

Yeats looked at his father, who nodded. Gran frowned but lifted her arms to allow Odysseus to jump down from her lap.

"Don't touch anything," Faith warned.

"Touch whatever you want," Gran countered.

"The house isn't safe, Mum," William said.

"Life isn't safe, William."

As he made for the door, his father suddenly grabbed his wrist. A line of sweat trickled down his face. "Don't take off that necklace, Yeats! It's important. Promise me!"

"I won't, Dad. I promise. And promise me you won't drink anymore when you're upset."

His father squeezed his eyes shut. "Never again, son. You have my word. Tastes awful anyway." They shared a rare, brief smile.

Before the door closed behind him he heard his

mother say, "You're scaring him, both of you! I've had enough of all this."

Yeats bit his nails as he plodded into the garden. The weekend could hardly be going worse. And now, banished outside, he couldn't even be a referee between his mother and father. He longed to be home, or anywhere else. But there was no getting away. His father's depression would come and go like clouds extinguishing the sun, following their family forever. The endless counseling sessions had not worked. The antidepressant drugs had failed. His mother and father were in the worst fight of his life. His mother was at her wit's end. And how could he blame her after what he had just heard?

Magic? Yeats sat heavily on a garden stone and covered his face. His heart thumped. His worst fears rose up like ghastly shadows and darkened his thoughts. His family would break apart for sure now. He could still hear his mother's skeptical voice.

His heart skipped again as another fear rushed over him. What Yeats had always believed was that his father suffered from a treatable depression. Now he saw it as something far deeper: his father was losing his mind. It was obvious. He acted childlike around Gran. He broke out in a sweat at the mere mention of Shari. Like old Mr. Sutcliff, his father was overwhelmed by tragedy and was slowly falling from reason. How long before he stopped cutting his hair and rang a bell for his tea? What would they do if his father lost his job at the university? Where would they go? Would he and his mother leave to let his father wallow in madness?

A tear squeezed out. It wasn't fair! Things were going well. Their house was in the middle of the street surrounded by kids his age and his school only a short distance away. Why did this have to happen now?

Yeats rubbed his eyes as a last specter loomed. Perhaps insanity ran in the family! His father, and now he learned his great-great-grandfather, were both completely loopy. Maybe it was only a matter of time before Yeats went mad as well. He saw his father's face again, white and sweating.

And then his mother's words echoed in his memory. *Your father is brilliant, Yeats. Don't let his gloomy clouds fool you. You have a right to be proud. I married an intelligent, kind, and handsome man. And our son is too.* She had not said anything like that for a long time.

Taking a breath, he looked around. He needed something to focus on, something to break up the adult banter and worrisome thoughts in his head. Gran's garden spread out in front of him.

Gran. What a character. And, yet, there was something comforting about her too. It felt good to have her hands on his shoulders. How could someone so strong, so clear, be caught up in a conversation about magic?

He glanced over the yard to where the fountain gaped open. With nothing better to do he made for it via an overgrown trail. Vines and mysterious shrubs spilled their dew on his jeans as he passed. Burrs scratched his T-shirt and he had to leap over a wicked little thorny bush.

He nearly banged into an old well but caught himself at the last moment. He put his hands on either side of the opening and peered into the darkness of the hole. The air rising from the deep was cool and damp. "Gran's old wishing well," he murmured, and the words echoed quietly back to him.

The mouth of the well looked rather grubby, with mottled lichens covering the inside as far as he could see. Despite his somber mood he grinned, for he realized his father might have stared down the same hole some twenty years before.

And then his frown returned. His father had said that his wish had not been granted. What did he mean? Was he alone at the time or was the girl with him? His frown deepened. Perhaps his father had wished for the girl to come back. Yeats leaned a little deeper into the well mouth. If that was the case, then the well was truly broken.

"I wish I knew what was going on," he added, more loudly than he had intended.

The moment his words were out he felt a tremor in his fingers, a ripple that stemmed from the cool stone and rattled up through his elbows. He felt the stones shake beneath his feet. From deep below came an ominous moan. His eyes widened, but he didn't let go of the fountain.

The moaning grew louder. Yeats caught his

breath when he heard a voice. It sounded like a boy.

Yeats tightened his grip. "Stay calm. It must be my echo," he assured himself. But the tone was different. It didn't sound exactly like his. And there was desperation in the voice. He could have sworn he heard someone say, "I wish! I wish!"

"Is anyone down there?" he asked experimentally. When there was no answer he took a deep breath. He squeezed his eyes shut and tried to think through the moans and trembling stones. He had said the words *I wish*, hadn't he? Perhaps the length or depth of the well tunnel could change the echo so that it sounded like someone else.

And then an idea popped into his head. It was a memory of standing at the state capitol fountain. His mother had said, "Make a wish, Yeats!" He remembered throwing something into the water.

Yeats let go of the well and dug into his pocket. He pulled out a penny. He held the coin briefly above the opening and then dropped it into the darkness. There was no splash or even so much as a tinkle. But the moan died instantly. The stones stopped shaking. There was complete silence for a moment. A crow cried raucously from a nearby tree.

"Weird," he murmured.

And then it happened. There was a muffled *boom* from below. Suddenly the ground began to shake so violently that Yeats was flung across the yawning mouth. His cheek scrunched against the stone. He fought blindly for a grip. His stomach dipped into the emptiness.

There was a succession of tiny low sounds and he felt pressure against his chest. Something was coming up the well. A second later the wind struck. It hit him like a gale, ripped his hands free, and blasted him into the bushes.

Dazed, he stared back at the well. From the wind a voice cried out, "I wish, I wish!" echoing a thousand times over. Tree branches blew straight up and leaves and twigs hurtled skyward in the volcanic debris.

Several of the stone slabs on the well mouth shook loose from their mortar and fell with a crash into the depths. The noise and wind stopped as suddenly as it had begun. A moment later the ground stopped shaking. Yeats stood slowly. The garden was quiet again, although, he noted, there were no birds chirping. Not after such a blast.

"Wow," he murmured softly. He stepped cautiously to the well and touched the cold stone with a quaking finger. Nothing happened. The well itself was now completely broken. It had gaping holes in the sides and the mouth was clogged with debris.

He was about to peer more closely when a sound caused him to turn his head toward the fountain. Only steps away, one of the tiles on the ground rocked on its edge, the scrape of stone on stone unmistakable in the silent garden. Then the movement stopped.

Yeats knelt and glanced around, wondering if Odysseus kept any feline company. But the cat was nowhere in sight. And no wonder. After the well's volcanic eruption he wouldn't wonder if Odysseus was attached to some tree trunk. "The well must have done this," he said. "Shaking up the ground and breaking the tiles with all its rumbling. I wonder if there is volcanic activity in the area?" The thought was somehow comforting in comparison to any mysterious alternatives. He sighed. It was just an earthquake. He glanced toward the house. Mom and Dad! They must have felt the earthquake too.

When no one rushed from the house, Yeats turned back to the tile. His hands were shaking. "Get a grip, Yeats," he scolded himself. "There's a simple explanation."

He gave the leaning tile a poke with his finger. Then he turned to the fountain. Some of it was blocked from view by vines and moss. The vegetation tore away easily after a few good tugs. He could see a basin now, and part of a pedestal. When a larger patch of moss broke free in his hands he suddenly came face-to-face with a gargoyle.

He fell backward, nearly landing on the broken tile. The leering face of the gargoyle was alarmingly close. He breathed a sigh of relief. It was only stone.

There was some writing cut into the smooth plane of the lip of the hideous face. The script was Gothic—hardly readable—and it trailed from one end of the creature's mouth to the other.

"'Come away, O human child,'" Yeats read. He scrambled to his knees. Scrubbing at the tree- and dirt-stained words with his sleeve, he uncovered more. "'To the waters and the wild. With a faery, hand in hand. For the world's more full of weeping than you can understand.'"

The scraping sound started up again, and Yeats turned quickly. He could see the broken tile better now and stretched out his hand to lift it. At the last second he retreated.

Can you, Yeats? Dare you, I wonder? Mr. Sutcliff's words echoed. Peering over the brush, Yeats saw Odysseus sitting up. Their eyes locked.

"I'm not scared, you know," Yeats challenged. The cat looked away.

The tile in the dirt was a thick slab of stone. Yeats prodded the raised edge. The stone scraped and ground as it leaned on its axis.

"There is something in there." Sunlight, miraculously finding a way through Gran's wilderness, glinted off an object in the dirt.

Don't touch anything!

Touch anything you want!

"I hope it's not bones." He imagined Hamlet, stooped at the grave, holding the jester's skull— something he'd seen in his dad's books. As he dug something poked his finger. A drop of blood dripped off his finger onto the earth.

There was something solid there, something metal. It had rounded edges and was not much longer than his hand.

The cat padded over stealthily, like a panther on the hunt. Yeats moved aside to let him sniff. The slab was too heavy for Odysseus. A second later his hackles were up and he hissed. Then abruptly he began to wash his leg.

Yeats stared from the cat to the hole, half expecting something to come out.

The sun disappeared behind clouds and the overhanging brush. Odysseus started on his second leg.

"What's wrong with you? You hiss, then you wash. You're a lot of help."

The object was heavy. It lay on a bed of earth, hastily scooped, for it only just fit the hole. After several tugs it slid out.

"A pirate!" Yeats exclaimed. It had a sea hat and cape, a cocky stance, one foot on a treasure chest and a sword in hand. A skull and crossbones grinned at Yeats from its hat. He turned the figure around. The fold of the cape provided a flat backing, as did the outflung sword arm. The elbow was worn.

"A bronze bookend," Yeats said. Odd—his father had just mentioned bookends. He wondered if there was a connection. He felt the hole for another bookend but it contained no further treasures. "You must be one of Grandfather Trafford's antiques," Yeats told the pirate. He turned the bookend over and read the words embossed on the back. "Gift House, New York. Eighteen twenty-six." He brushed off the soil as the first drops of rain fell. "Let's take you inside, Captain."

The kitchen was empty. Hefting the bookend, he paused. From the hallway leading to the stairs he thought he heard his mother, although the tricky nature of the house made him uncertain. He stood undecided between the kitchen and the hall.

Odysseus gave a yowl.

Yeats saw it too. The door to the back room was

ajar. "Dad?" he murmured. The pirate suddenly grew very heavy as he approached the door. He almost dropped it.

"You see that?" Yeats whispered. The cat curled around his legs, tugging. "All right, all right. Don't have a fur ball. We'll have a look."

Odysseus slipped into the gloom.

"Wait!" Yeats leaned against the door frame, undecided. Other than the steady rhythm of a clock the room was quiet.

"Psssssst, pssssst," he called. "Odysseus! Come here." His blood pounded in an ominous rhythm. A bookshelf inconveniently blocked further view into the room. Papers scattered inside and Yeats jumped back. The pirate's head smacked the door frame.

"Stupid cat's made a mess. And they're going to think I did it." With a last look at the kitchen Yeats stepped into the gloom.

5

ARABIAN
DAYS

Upstairs, Mr. Sutcliff rose from his chair for a second time that morning. William stood in the doorway as shakily as his son had earlier, along with his mother and what must be his wife. The old man smiled.

"William."

Twenty years were suspended between them.

"Mr. Sutcliff, sir."

"You have come back."

"Yes, sir. I have."

"Your appearance freezes my blood." He lifted his pipe weakly. "Then again, I must look frightful to you too."

William shifted his feet. He cast a glance around

his old room. Shari used to sit on the window seat. "You're looking well, Mr. Sutcliff."

The old man grunted. "I met Yeats. A fine boy. Strapping young lad."

William squared his shoulders. "We're very proud of him. It hasn't been easy. But I've made a life. And Yeats has done well. He's overprotective, at times, trying to make up for my episodes."

"I can't imagine." Mr. Sutcliff shook his head.

"I can't bring her back, sir."

"Can't?" Mr. Sutcliff gave a sidelong glance. "Or won't?"

"No." William shook his head. "I tried for years. I can't remember enough. I lost six months of memory, a year in the hospital after that. Everyone thought I was crazy. *I* thought I was crazy. I've been on antidepressants ever since."

Faith watched both men closely.

Mr. Sutcliff squeezed his eyes shut. "That is all, is it?" He clasped his pipe to his chest and murmured:

"'Knowing my heart's best treasure was no more;

That neither present time, nor years unborn . . .'"

William finished the stanza. "'. . . Could to my sight that heavenly face restore.' William Wordsworth, 'Surprised by Joy.'"

Mr. Sutcliff shut his eyes.

Gran swept past her son and daughter-in-law and helped the old man into his chair. "Don't give up hope, dear Mr. Sutcliff. You and I are poets. We allow ourselves a little melancholy. But these children love stories. Shari loved stories. So did William. Solid, wise literature, full of adventure and the greatest of all ingredients . . . hope. I have not met a child's story yet that did not offer it somewhere. Surely in this house there are doors that can be opened again to bring Shari home."

"I've spent days in the library!" Mr. Sutcliff moaned. "Nothing so much as a whisper. Only the silly bookend can't keep still. And he won't talk."

Faith shook her head.

"Bookend?" William repeated. He tapped his forehead. "That's important."

Mr. Sutcliff nodded silently. He closed his eyes.

"Poor man," Faith murmured.

"We'll need to revisit the library," said Gran. "Perhaps something will trigger your memory."

"Oh, it's in the library, all right," said William. "I just don't remember what it was." He avoided his wife's eyes. "Something my great-grandfather put there. Something very powerful."

"I've ransacked that room," Gran said. "But I'll look again. And you should too, William. We need a clue."

William's voice was strained. "The bookends. Mum, when you mentioned them something stirred in my memory."

"What are you suggesting?" Faith asked. She kept glancing from Mr. Sutcliff to her husband.

"Nothing, yet."

"Of course it's the bookends," Mr. Sutcliff muttered. "Their magic is manifest in the library somehow. And don't discount the wishing well, broken as it is! Philip Trafford would have known. But he took all his secrets with him!"

"The well does not work," William muttered. "I wished a thousand times and the wishes just swirled around but never came out."

"Oh, dear," Faith whispered.

About to turn, William suddenly stopped. "Have you read Collfield's unexpurgated version of the *Arabian Nights*, sir?"

Mr. Sutcliff nodded somberly. "Dangerous book. I cannot think of a more volatile, intelligent, exotic setting than that."

"Why do you keep on about this book, and the library, and a bunch of bookends?" Faith looked at each of them. "I have been told that William and Shari were on an adventure one day when they were attacked. Attacked by *men*! Real people, somewhere on this property. You are scaring me. Thank God Yeats isn't here."

Walking stiffly to his bed, Mr. Sutcliff picked up the book. He held it out to Faith. "This is only a copy of the one in the library." He ruffled its pages. "Hot sun and sand by day. Sweat and filth consume the streets. Steal an orange, lose a hand. The wealth and wisdom and science of the upper class are uncontested in the world." He took a step closer. "She would have to use her cunning, all her strength, to stay alive in a place like that. And who brought her there, hmmm? *Who?* Unconscionable villains!" A tear rolled down his cheek. He stumbled.

"Help him, William," Faith directed.

"All her abilities," said the old man as they laid him down. William gasped when Mr. Sutcliff suddenly gripped his hand. "Will it be enough?"

6

COLLFIELD'S
UNEXPURGATED TRANSLATION

A large window overlooking the garden provided what little light there was in Gran's library. Books on tall shelves reached the ceiling; short shelves and tables were cluttered with volumes. Must and decay reminded Yeats of old museums he had visited.

"Dad?" he whispered. The room was long. Hundreds of books seemed to suck the sound away. Odysseus's tail vanished around a column. Yeats paused. He hefted the pirate.

"Odysseus!" Yeats hissed and took two more steps. The girl had disappeared from this room, according to the adults. But they hadn't settled on how. Magic, perhaps. It was just the place for that sort of thing.

And then he saw the cat.

Odysseus was poised to strike, his fur bristling, eyes focused on a narrow bookcase only a few feet away. Hidden under a protruding set of rotting encyclopedias, only the side and carved feet of the bookcase were visible.

"Stop that!" Yeats's voice cracked.

Odysseus ran between the boy's feet, still spitting and hissing.

"Watch it, Odysseus! You're getting in the way." Cat and boy tangled and Yeats stumbled. In an effort to protect the pirate bookend Yeats rolled onto his shoulder. He lay on his back staring at the bookshelf. Several books protruded from under the legs of the bottom shelf. *Paradise Lost, The Tempest, The Adventures of Tom Sawyer.*

He tried to sit, but the pirate upset his balance. He set the pirate at the near end of the bookcase and knelt in front of the shelf. And then he saw it. On the same shelf, yet at the opposite end, was a book. ". . . the *Arabian Nights: The Marvels and Wonders of the Thousand and One Nights*. His heart gave a disturbing thump when he read the next part. *Collfield's unexpurgated translation*. He touched the leather binding.

Then he noticed something else. He peeked around the book. The tall volume shielded a second pirate, identical to his, back-to-back with the book. There were other books as well, but they had fallen behind the shelf. "Did you do this?" he asked Odysseus. The cat settled on the back of Yeats's legs. "Bold face, no bite. A lot of good you are."

Odysseus stared hard. Turning back to the *Arabian Nights,* Yeats suddenly caught his breath. The bookend he had found in the garden was now only a foot from the *Arabian Nights*. He pushed the cat off his legs. He must have moved the pirate when he looked at Odysseus, he assured himself. He glanced at the door. He could run to it in a second if he needed to.

Collfield's translation was covered in dust and was the oldest-looking of all the volumes. Yeats slid the book from the shelf, raising a cloud of dust. He sneezed and the book fell open at his knees.

It is told in days of long ago, that once there lived a king in the lands of India and China and lands between, who was great in strength and wealth.

Yeats sneezed again and the pages flipped. *And lo! Shaharazad saw that the dawn was coming and with her lord's permission she ceased her storytelling with the promise of more the following night. The king slept without the torment of his nightly dreams and awoke with a fresh vision of his kingdom.* The letters were in a rather fancy font, and Yeats traced the elaborately decorated *A* at the top of the page.

"He's in!" said a voice, alarmingly close. Yeats's fingers dug into the pages. The voice continued. "*Where* have ye been? It's been twenty years if'n ye hadn't noticed."

The voice was coming from the bookshelf. One of the bookend pirates had removed his metal foot from his treasure chest and was dusting off his sea cape. The second pirate stared at Yeats.

"He's not in yet, ye stupid blowfish!"

The first pirate whipped his foot back onto the chest and resumed his pose.

Yeats ran out of air. The book fell to the floor.

"Hold yer pose," the first pirate whispered. The second pirate raised his steely eyebrows.

"Too late."

"Hold yer pose!"

"Too late. He's lookin'."

"Huuuuhhh," wheezed Yeats.

"Son of a sea dog! What do we do now?"

The pirate walked off his platform and over to Yeats. For the first time Yeats realized that this pirate was different from the pirate he had found outside. The pirate from the garden wore tall sea boots, whereas this pirate was missing a leg. In its place was a wooden peg. The peg leg made the pirate stoop a little when he walked but did not interfere with his speed.

"Ye little shred of rotten seaweed . . ."

"Shut up, Skin!" shouted the boot-wearing pirate. He threw his hands up and stepped down from the shelf. "It's not his fault! Argh! Right back into the thick of it the moment I'm back."

Yeats leaned as far from the shelf as his limbs would allow.

"Shut it yerself, Bones," challenged Skin, the peg-legged pirate.

"Help," gasped Yeats.

Bones eyed him up and down and grimaced. "I suppose we'll have to, now."

Skin drew his sword. "Ye were in!" he accused Yeats. "Swear it! It weren't me. Ye was reading! Ye can't see or hear us when ye is reading." He stomped his peg leg angrily.

"I . . . I stopped reading," Yeats whispered. "I was looking at the letters."

"It *was* yer fault," Bones said to the fiery Skin. Bones eased Skin's sword down.

Then Skin raised the weapon again swiftly. "Pick up that book and start reading!"

His heart pounding, Yeats managed, "Why?"

"Impudence! Scurvy dog! Dirty . . . er . . . dirty . . . er . . ."

"Rat?" Yeats offered.

"Rat!" Skin spat and pointed his sword at Yeats's nose.

"Put that away!" Bones ordered. He scratched his unshaven chin. "Skulls and crossbones, I need to think! I carry the brains for us both. When it be time for muscle I'll let ye know. We've precious little time afore someone else walks in."

Yeats glanced furtively, expecting some new specter from the bookstacks. "Who?"

"Yer own meddling kind, that's who!" Skin said. "I shouldn't wonder if old Sutcliff makes an appearance at any moment."

"Mr. Sutcliff?"

"I've had trouble with him." Skin shifted uncomfortably. He made a little circle in the dust with the end of his peg. "He knows about us."

"What happened?" asked Bones.

"He spies on me! He caught me whistling a few times and singing a sea chantey. But I never—I swear it on my granny's boots—I never granted him a wish!" The pirate clapped his hands over his mouth the moment the words were out.

There was a long pause. "That weren't a wise thing to say, partner," Bones said with a grimace.

He slapped his forehead. "Not surprising, mind ye, since ye've got as much wit as a stone!"

Intuitively Yeats pounced. He gripped the closest pirate, who happened to be Bones, around the waist. The pirate thrashed his legs and pounded his little fists on Yeats's finger.

Yeats raised him level to his eyes yet far enough away so that he could not be poked by the pirate's sword. "A wish?" he demanded. "I get a wish?"

The pirate scowled back, then threw up his hands. "Open yer hand, landlubber! I can't run for it. Ye've asked the golden question. Now I've got to answer." He shot an angry look at his partner and said, "Ye be one of the finest idiots I've known." Skin hung his head.

Hesitantly Yeats opened his fist. Removing his hat, Bones sat heavily on Yeats's palm.

"A fine fix we're in again," he grumbled.

"Well?" prodded Yeats. He rose to his knees and took a better look at the pirate. "You know about my dad, don't you? And Shari. You're the magical . . . whatevers . . . Gran and Dad talked about."

"Bookends," said Bones. "We're bookends. And don't get yer hackles up." He rested his hand on his sword.

Yeats snorted. "Try it. I don't care if you're made of metal. I'll kick you across the room like a football."

"Simmer down, codfish!" said Skin. "Ye be as flighty as a . . . er . . . as a . . ."

"Pigeon," Yeats filled in.

"Exactly."

"Listen, you metal clowns," Yeats growled. "I want to help my dad. My family's falling apart. So, if you're the cause of it, and you know how to fix it, tell me now!" He raised his fist.

Skin rested his peg leg on the edge of a book and picked at his nails with a dagger. "A touch jumpy, are we? The 'metal clowns' bit was good, though. Very witty."

"You start talking or I'll knock over this bookshelf. Then I'll tell everyone in this house— no—I'll tell the whole world about you! Then you'll have more explaining to do."

Skin and Bones exchanged glances. "Will ye,

now?" they chimed simultaneously, with chilling calm.

"Yes," said Yeats. "Now what's all this about a wish?"

Bones sighed. Then he said simply, "If we're caught using our magic then ye gets one wish." The bristles of his metal mustache twitched.

"A wish," Yeats repeated.

"Aye."

Odysseus rubbed against Yeats's leg. "Are you suggesting," asked Yeats, "that I can ask for a wish . . . as in a fairy-tale kind of wish? Like a genie?"

"That's the idea."

"Anything?"

"No," said the pirate. "Can't bring the dead back to life. And the wish has to come from here." He swept a hand around the shelves.

"What do you mean? I can't leave the library?"

"No! Ye can go anywhere a book goes."

"Why?"

"Our magic is limited to books!" Skin shouted.

"Why?" asked Yeats.

"Because we're BOOKENDS!" cried Skin. He rolled his eyes and tapped his forehead.

"Oh," said Yeats. "Fair enough." He frowned. "Does that mean I can ask for anything inside a book? Like all the treasure from Treasure Island?"

Bones shook his head. "Can't take things out of books. Ye can only go inside. And ye can come back out."

Thoughts were swirling in his head so fast that Yeats could hardly think. "So I can go inside any book I want?"

"Aye."

"Wow." Yeats's mind was flooded with possibilities. He knew a lot of good stories! *Peter Pan*. He could go to Neverland! *Robin Hood*. Fighting the Sheriff of Nottingham with a quarter staff. Wa-hoo!

The pirates waited impatiently. He shook his head vigorously to clear his mind. "Wait, wait a minute," he murmured. "This is what happened to Shari, isn't it?" His eyes widened as the truth struck home. "She made a wish, didn't she?"

Skin and Bones nodded. Yeats's gaze dropped

to the book on the floor. "She wished to be in the *Arabian Nights*!"

"Aye," said Bones. "More to the point, she wished to be Shaharazad."

All the glorious possibilities drained away as Yeats imagined his father's desperate face. "What did my dad wish for?" he murmured.

Bones covered his heart with his hat. "He wished to be with her. Very honorable, I'll give him that. Then, not long after they were in the story, he broke the spell and came back."

"Why? How?"

The pirate snapped his fingers at Yeats's eyes. "Would ye mind settin' a poor old man down for a moment? To get me balance?"

Yeats regripped and said vehemently, "No way!"

"All right, all right," grumbled the pirate.

"How did my dad break the spell?" Yeats repeated. "And why?"

Bones rested his sword arm on Yeats's thumb. "Spells are meant to be broken," the pirate said. "That's the way of magic. It don't last. But ye've got to want it with all yer heart—more than anything else—before it will break. Yer dad wanted to come home. And he wanted the girl to go with him."

"But she wouldn't," Yeats said softly. "Because her parents were dead. Because she was searching for a happy ending."

"Ye can't wish for another person," said Bones. "Only yerself. Yer father had to come back alone. And in the nick of time too. He was about to lose his head!"

Yeats looked around the room and thought of the books, the history and stories, and all the glorious worlds he had read since he was little. His father had stood in the same place twenty years ago. But he was not alone back then. And the story was chosen by Shari. The result of that wish had left old Mr. Sutcliff unstable, his father in a lifelong depression, and his family on the brink of splitting.

Yeats scowled. He knew what he had to wish for. But before he said the words he needed answers to a few questions.

"If I asked, could you take me to Shari?" he asked.

"Aye," said Bones.

"And if I could convince her to go with me, would the spell be broken and she could return?"

The pirates regarded each other. Finally Bones shrugged and said, "If she wants to come back here with her whole heart . . . then yes."

Yeats leaned eagerly forward.

"But it gets muddy in the story world, lad," Bones added. "It will be hard to think clearly as ye do now. Especially for the girl. She's been in for a long time! Her memory will be like a cloudy soup."

Yeats squeezed his eyes shut. "Is there a chance I could get stuck in there too?"

"Aye," they said together.

"I don't like the sound of that," said Yeats.

"'Course ye don't," jeered Skin. "Ye be as lily-livered as yer father."

Yeats turned red and scowled as fiercely as any pirate. "Say that again, Skinny, and I'll chase your boogers up your nose with your own sword."

Skin hopped up from his sitting position and swung his sword. "I'll kill him! Davy Jones, I don't care. Just let me kill him."

Bones thrust his finger at Yeats. "Say yer sorry!"

"No!"

"This isn't going to help yer father. Say it!"

Yeats pounded the top of the shelf, bouncing Skin off balance.

"Sorry," Yeats said through gritted teeth. "Sorry," he said again. "But don't you ever call my dad a coward."

Skin regarded him closely for a moment before putting away his sword. "A sword up the nose, eh? Very pirate-like. Might use it meself."

Yeats took a deep breath and regained his composure. "Will you help me if I get stuck?"

"Why should we?" Bones retorted. "Not like we owe ye or yer father anything! The codfish! Hauled me off to the garden when the girl didn't come back. Demanded more wishes to go back and get her."

The sudden image of his father as a frightened boy filled Yeats with rage. "You didn't help him?

He needed you! That's disgusting, even for a pirate."

"I've been eating garden dirt for twenty years," Bones retorted. "I suppose I paid for it by being marooned."

"Well, if you're so hostile to my father, then why are you answering my questions?" Yeats shot back.

"We have to," answered Skin sulkily. "There's a certain rotting fairness built in to the magic. Gives ye yer chance. Questions come before the wish."

Yeats rubbed a hand over his eyes. He had to think. The magic of the house was beyond reckoning; it tore down his defenses and left him numb. No wonder his father was depressed! He had to live in the logical world of the university while knowing what had happened in this room defied common sense.

But at least his father was not crazy.

The pirate's gravelly voice broke into his thoughts. "So, lad. It's up to ye. I've been away for twenty years and have lots to do. Let's get on with it. Time to make a wish."

7

THE SEA
OF WORDS

Although it was his first time in the library, Yeats felt a strong connection to the place. He was loath to make his wish and leave. In the library, his father, mother, and even Gran were only a shout away. And it didn't help knowing that one other person who had been in his position had never returned.

He rubbed the back of his neck and touched his father's necklace. The bell made a faint tinkle. That gave him the courage he needed. Yeats squared his shoulders and sat up straight. "I'm ready," he said.

Bones smacked his hand. "Open yer fist," he commanded. Now that it had come to the

moment, Yeats knew instinctively he could release the pirate. He set him down beside his partner.

"Ye can't change a wish partway," Bones instructed.

"A wish is final," Skin added with a snarl.

"Occasionally there's a wind when the story world opens," Bones said. "Don't mind it! And don't shout. Focus on the words!"

"What words?" Yeats's voice cracked.

"Are ye daft? Ye've got to be reading the book in order to get there. Now pick it up."

Yeats reached for the *Arabian Nights*. His hands shook as he placed it on his lap.

The pirates raised their swords and pointed them at Yeats's nose. "Now, lad!" they cried. "What be yer wish?"

Yeats was about to ask that they take him to Shari when a thought suddenly struck him. He needed to see her alone. Someone had taken Shari when she and his father had first come to the story. Gran called them "abductors." They could still be around. Yeats wiped away a bead of sweat. "I wish for you to take me to Shaharazad where she is alone!"

He squeezed his eyes shut. He waited but nothing happened. He felt Odysseus's warm side against his legs. One of the pirates coughed. When he opened his eyes Bones was tapping his sword impatiently on the shelf. The pirate indicated the book. "Read!"

"Oh!" Yeats exclaimed. "I forgot." Once again he mustered his strength. "For Dad," he whispered. "This is for Dad." He flipped a page or two and began to read.

Shaharazad was the eldest of the vizier's daughters. She devoted herself to poetry and stories, studying the books and lessons of the past.

An image of the pretty, determined girl from the picture in Gran's kitchen popped into his head. *Many books had been gathered to the palace and the girl rigorously attended to the wisdom of the wise and the history of peoples all over the world. By day, she recited poetry and basked in the treasures of stories long forgotten by all but the poets and minstrels.*

In the corners of his eyes the library blurred. Odysseus pushed hard against his legs. A wind tore through the stacks and the pages of the book flapped. He felt dizzy and his hair blew wildly.

"Hello, matey!" Bones shouted. The library was gone. They were in a rowboat shrouded by cloud. Skin, as large as life, sat at the tiller. Oars creaked. They rose and fell with the swells under the canopy of early dawn.

"Where are we?" Yeats whispered. He clung to the sides of the boat. The air was damp and free of salt. Green water lapped against the hull.

"Where do you think?" Skin snapped. "We're on the sea of words." He was much more alarming in human size. Neither pirate's skin was metallic anymore. Now, every feature of the flesh-and-blood buccaneers stood out in the dim light, from their stubbly beards to the tattoos laced around their arms. Bones looked more tattered than Skin. There was a hole in his hat and his face was darker and deeply tanned. His sword, too, was pockmarked. But then again, he had been outside for the last twenty years. Erosion had taken its toll.

"It doesn't smell like ocean," said Yeats. Rather, the air smelled musty and reminiscent of Gran's library.

"It will," said Bones. "We haven't made harbor yet. Hold on!" he yelled.

Something butted against the bottom of the boat. They lurched and Skin gripped the gunwale, grinning. "I love the small stuff."

Yeats peered into the bubbling green sea. "What is it?"

"Words," puffed Bones.

"We're rowing through words?" Yeats exclaimed. He caught sight of black shapes rolling through the water. And to think that his father had traveled in the same boat!

"'Course!" Skin cranked hard on the tiller. "Small print. It's an old book!"

"I don't understand," said Yeats.

"We be skimmin' pages," said the pirate. "We haven't committed yet. When we commit to a chapter then ye'll smell the sea. Then we'll weigh anchor and ye can talk to the girl."

Odysseus's claws were fully embedded in Yeats's sock. Yeats untangled the cat and put him on his lap. The book, he noted, was gone.

"That's the second time that mangy beast has

come for a ride." Bones pointed to the cat. "He came with the girl and yer father too. Seems he can't grow old till the young lass comes back."

"No wonder Dad was surprised to see you!" Yeats said to Odysseus. "You must be the world's oldest cat!"

Mist poured over the bow and brushed past Yeats's face in whimpers and whispers.

Yeats swatted at the clouds. "What is that?"

"Echoes from the story world," Bones answered. "Ye'll hear more of it. We're just past the introduction." He leaned into the oars with practiced ease, his muscles bulging under his shirt. Skin sang an old chantey:

"So swab the decks and reef the sails!

Hold ye hats and mind the gale.

We're off to San Francisco!"

His singing voice was gravelly, just as Yeats imagined it would be, yet also strong and wild. His peg leg scraped against the bottom of the boat with each swell. Yeats was certain, bookends or no, they were capable of handling themselves in a fight.

A few minutes later Yeats's skin tingled and a thrilling sensation rippled through his body. He sucked in the musty breeze and instantly felt brave and strong like a warrior.

"Hurrah!" he shouted. Seconds later he cowered on all fours, terrified to look over the side. "What is happening to me?" Yeats gasped.

"It's normal for a first voyage!" Bones assured him. Yeats clutched Odysseus. Bones rested his oars. "We're passing through Chapter One. Ye be sensing all the emotions. Be thankful we aren't traveling too far."

Yeats felt his strength returning. Suddenly, without knowing why, he cupped his hands around his mouth and burst into the national anthem. His voice did not sound anything like Skin's, but he didn't mind. He sensed hundreds of people watching his performance and he put his arms out to them.

Skin snorted and Yeats felt silly. The feelings kept roaring through him. Panic struck his heart like a fist.

"When will this stop?" he gasped.

"Fight it," said Skin.

"How?" he groaned.

"Think of one thing and the rest will go."

"One thing, one thing," he muttered as the panic rose. Yeats grabbed his necklace. The marble was smooth and cool and when the bell tinkled he thought of his father's concerned face. "I am here for Dad," he murmured. "I'm on a rescue mission." He squeezed his eyes shut. A wave of terror washed over him. Just then, a monster welled up in his mind, but he pushed it back with the words, "I'm going to rescue Shari and bring her back." The panic subsided, melting away as quickly as it had come.

Yeats shuddered. He needed to stay focused. Talking seemed to help. "How do we break the spell?" he asked. "How do we get Shari to remember who she is?"

"We?" Skin frowned. "Not *we*. Ye."

Bones growled, "I told ye that in the library! We're finished with our end of the bargain soon as we weigh anchor. Enough questions!"

Yeats shook off a wave of giddy laughter by

murmuring, "My dad is depressed; my dad is depressed." Out loud he said, "Fine. How do I break the spell?"

The pirates said nothing.

"Well?"

"We've answered all we have to," said Skin. "Now that we're on the way."

"Oh, I get it," said Yeats. "Now that I've made my wish you don't have to help me with anything else."

Still the pirates said nothing. Skin squinted menacingly.

Now more than ever Yeats needed answers, before his escorts fulfilled their magical obligations and "weighed anchor." "Hey, Skin," Yeats said. "Want to know a really good pirate insult? I mean one that will curdle people's blood, they'll be so mad? It's very witty."

Skin squirmed.

"I know some nasty ones," Yeats added.

The pirate could not contain himself. "Tell me!"

Yeats smiled and looked at the sea. "No. Not unless you answer a few more questions."

"Not fair!" shouted the pirate.

"That's right," retorted Yeats.

"Come on, lad," said Skin. "Be nice now. I could use a little wit."

"Huh!" grunted Bones in agreement.

"All right," said Skin. "I propose a swap. An insult for an answer."

"Done!" agreed Yeats.

"Ye both be daft," muttered Bones.

"Let's begin," said Yeats. Skin sat poised. Yeats scowled and said, "If courage was measured by the length of your sword, you'd be wearing a sewing needle."

There was a pause while the pirate digested the insult. When it finally sunk in, his hands began to shake and his face twisted with wrath. He reached for his sword.

Yeats leaned as far back as possible, but there was nowhere to go other than over the side. All of a sudden, Skin gave a great guffaw and slapped his knee. "Good, good! That got me. And I was going to kill ye!"

Yeats blanched. He swallowed hard and then

asked his first question. "How do I undo Shari's wish?"

Bones glared at his partner but did not interfere when Skin answered, "Ye must make her want for something outside the story world, from her home world. She must remember who she was and wish to be herself again with all her heart. Names, places, anything might help her drain the bilge of the last twenty years. Objects seem to work best— favorite childhood toys, a stuffed animal, that sort of thing."

Yeats nodded. He would be a stranger to her, but he could certainly tell her about his father. And her grandfather and Gran. Even Gran's house. If only he had a picture!

Skin looked at him expectantly. "Come on, lad," he said. "Another insult."

Yeats shuffled as far from the pirate as he could. Then he cleared his throat. "I've seen better mustaches after a glass of milk," he said.

The pirate twirled the ends of his mustache agitatedly. The insult had obviously been effective, for Skin leaned menacingly toward Yeats one second then forced himself back to the tiller the next. When he was in command of himself he gasped, "I like that one too. What's the question?"

Yeats chewed his lip. He knew there were many questions to ask that would be helpful, but which were the most important? "Who will I be in the story?" he asked finally.

"Yerself," said Skin. "Ye did not ask to be a character."

"But won't I look strange? I mean, it's the land of Arabia. From a long time ago."

"That's another question," said Skin. "Insult me please."

While thinking of insults was tiresome, the present company greatly aided inspiration. "You're such a pathetic pirate," Yeats said, "the insignia on your flag should show a puppy holding a rose instead of a skull and crossbones."

Bones stopped rowing. Skin bared his teeth. "Ye insulted the Jolly Roger," he growled. "That's going too far."

"No I didn't," answered Yeats quickly. "I said, *'you* are so pathetic.'"

Bones looked at Skin and shrugged. "Fair point."

"What be the next question?" asked Skin.

Yeats considered. He needed to load the question, at least a two for one. "How can I do what I need to do in order to rescue Shari when I am still me and not one of the characters and I don't even speak Arabic?"

Skin stared back blankly, then said to his partner, "That be a bit of a mouthful for me. What say ye?"

"There are thousands of unwritten characters in any book," said Bones to Yeats. "Ye'll find yer way. Make use of yer wits," he said and then winked, "like ye've done with us, and lose yerself in the crowd. And why would ye need to speak Arabic? This book is written in English!"

Suddenly, a large patch of mist loomed over the bow. An enormous mouth yawned in front of Yeats and snapped viciously at his face. It exploded into wisps, which burst against his forehead. He swallowed a scream.

Skin smirked. "Welcome to the story world. Ye looked as white as . . . as . . . a chicken!"

When his breath returned, Yeats said, "Not bad. You're getting wittier."

Skin doffed his hat.

"But," Yeats added, "your legs are so skinny and your head is so fat that you look more like an overgrown turnip wearing pajamas than a pirate."

Skin lunged and the boat keeled over hard to starboard. Yeats would have fallen out if Bones hadn't caught him. Odysseus was permanently attached to the gunwales, his claws dug in like spikes. When the boat righted everyone fell back into place.

"Enough! No more insults!" Bones roared. He adjusted his hat. "We've got a wish to fulfill. And we are almost there."

"Wait!" protested Yeats. "You've got to answer my question, especially after the last insult. Come on, Skin."

The pirate shrugged. "Well, it were a good one, I'll give ye that."

Without hesitating Yeats asked, "How will I recognize her? I mean, it's been years, so she will look completely different."

"Oh, ye'll find yer girlie-friend, all right," said Skin.

Yeats grimaced. "She's not my girlfriend. She's my father's age!"

"Oh no she's not! She's the same age as when she entered the book. And that answer was free. Just 'cause I'm a bit of a romantic." He winked knowingly.

"Land ho!" Bones hollered.

The musty smell that had surrounded them on the sea of words disappeared and in its place blew a fresh wind. A seabird cried overhead. The shrouds thinned out and the warm hues of sunset filled the sky.

"Make ready for landing!" Bones said. A shore appeared. Low mountains the color of sand and without a speck of green rose through the mist in the distance. Before the foothills, a vast desert stretched toward them. The air rippled with heat, and for the first time the smell of the ocean came fresh on the wind. Other smells competed with the brine: oranges and spice, and something sickeningly sweet like overripe garbage.

Gardens and fruit groves came into view. They were latticed along the desert and ran along a silver river that sparkled with the last rays of the sunset. It wound from the mountains, cutting through farmlands and ending at a magnificent sight: a spiral-towered city with glistening white walls. Gold reflected off the tops of the highest towers. Small boats and punts drifted in a congested mass at the headland.

Staying clear of the river's mouth, the pirates made for a secluded beach. The pungent odor of lemons and limes and fresh mint overwhelmed the salty wind. Lush gardens breathed cool air in their faces and the stark desert disappeared behind the dunes.

The pirates ran the boat aground and leapt ashore. Yeats leaned over the side, a little fearful of getting out of the boat, and grabbed a fistful of beach. Its whiteness reminded him of beaches his family had visited during his father's revitalization trips. The memory of his father made him stand. He set Odysseus down on the bench. "Stay here," he commanded. Odysseus stared back uncertainly.

"I know. I'm scared too." He scratched the cat's ears. "But I need you to watch these pirates. It's going to be scary out there," Yeats said and nodded in the direction of the palace. "You keep these bookends honest for me. If they've been lying in any way, knock them off their shelf for me."

Skin did not laugh. Instead, he eyed the cat warily.

Yeats took a deep breath. "So, this is it," he said. Both pirates nodded. "All right then," Yeats said. He put on his best scowl and stepped onto the beach.

8

THE
VIZIER'S DAUGHTER

The sand was cool and real enough. Yeats took a good look around. "Where are we? Or do I need to give you an insult first?"

Bones glanced over at Skin, who, at the mention of insults, looked up eagerly. "No," Bones said quickly. "No more insults. I'll tell ye. We be at the king's summer palace. The back entrance. Nobody here at this time of day."

Yeats frowned. "Are you visible to the people here?"

"Aye. At the moment, we're in the story too."

Interesting, thought Yeats. "Why did you bring me to this spot? Isn't Shaharazad the vizier's daughter—wouldn't she be at home?"

Skin fixed him with an impatient glare. "Would ye go anywhere without yer adviser if ye lived in a land where every one of yer sons competed for yer throne and might cut yer throat to take it?"

"I suppose not."

"Night's coming," Bones said. "Ye'd best get on with it. Steal inside and ye'll find her quick. She'll be in the garden. And keep a wary eye out for palace guards. They be the ones that almost took ye father's head!"

Yeats blanched at the thought. "Could you wait for me?" he pleaded. "I'll try and be quick."

"No!" they chimed.

"You're sure I can get back?" Yeats looked from one to the other.

Bones doffed his hat. "Ye have my word as a pirate and as a bookend." Then he added, "As long as ye break the wish."

Desperate, Yeats added to Skin, "If you come when I need you I'll give you a year's worth of insults. I'll insult you all day long."

"Get on with ye," Bones said gruffly before his partner could reply. "I've had enough. What ye seek and made yer wish for is through that gate. We've done our part. Now if ye want to help yer father, ye best be about yer business and we'll be about ours."

Yeats watched Bones get on board. He wondered if he'd made a dreadful mistake after all and if it was the last time he would see them. Or worse, if it was the last time he would see anyone he knew from his own world. Odysseus peered over the rail in mournful salute. Although the pirates could hardly be called friendly, they were the last link to Yeats's parents and anything he could call home.

"Anchor away!" called Bones.

Skin pushed the boat off the beach and jumped in. The boat slipped out into the waves and Bones began his steady pull on the oars. They quickly drew away from the shore. Yeats remained frozen on the sand. From across the water he could hear Skin singing his song again.

"Use your wits," Yeats murmured. Tempted to wave, he turned quickly from the sea before they vanished.

Hands on hips, Yeats surveyed the land. Up

at the top of the dune there was a gate in the palace wall as the pirates had said, and beyond it a garden. On the warm, dry wind the scent of sweet blossoms filled the air. Although his heart thumped briskly, his curiosity and sense of adventure started to take over. He fixed his scowl again and faced the new world.

Royalty would seek solace in a place that smelled of blossoms, not garbage, he reasoned. He shrugged and followed his nose.

His feet sank into sand as he trudged toward the palace. At the top of the beach his vantage point changed and he had a better sense of the place.

Walls separated the poor from the wealthy. The palace and gardens were cut off from the sea and port town. The walls were whitewashed, baked clay, and loomed higher then he could throw a stone. The heat emanating from the brick was stifling. But the artistry and majesty of the place quickly diverted him from his discomfort. Colored tiles formed a mosaic of a roaring jackal beside the gate, and running along the highest wall was a border of flowing script as tall as Yeats. The stone was pockmarked and scored by the elements. The walls continued as far as he could see.

The city was bristling with activity on land and water, with bazaars, markets, churches, soldiers, peasants, and animals everywhere. His scowl deepened. In the city he could at least blend into crowds and search with some anonymity. But not here at the palace—not without a disguise. He sat with his back to the gate and waited for night. The darkness would be his cloak. When the shades of night finally came down and he could wait no longer, he stood up.

The gate creaked open to reveal a starlit garden. It was nothing like the jumbled mess of Gran's garden. A path of white stones formed a large oval around neatly tilled beds of blooming plants and cultivated trees. The smell of freshly turned soil wafted on the night air. And there were voices.

The moon shed its cover, opening the garden as light to a page. Two figures stood on the central path, an old man and a girl.

"You must tell me, Mohassin. I beseech you!" the girl said.

The old man's voice trembled. "My lady, I cannot. Your father, the vizier, has made each of us swear, on the tombs of our fathers no less, that we will not breach our silence on this matter. You endanger your servants to ask that question."

Yeats listened intently.

The girl sighed. "What would you have me do? Every morning I hear wailing outside the palace. Night after night I hear their cries! The voices of mothers and sisters and daughters. Upon my soul, Mohassin, I will find out."

"My lady. You must shut your ears and close your eyes."

"I cannot!"

The old man sighed. "Your people love you, my lady. And with discretion"—his voice trembled—"I dare say, not a princess in this land shares your love and duty to the people."

"And I will not rest while the city weeps," the girl replied.

"Punish as you may. There is nothing that can move me."

The girl's voice broke. "Go, Mohassin! I will

not be the cause of grief to such a friend. Go back
to your kitchen without fear and take these coins
for your trouble."

"Dear lady. Your kindness is enough."

The figures parted and the servant hobbled
to a set of steps leading to a colonnade. The girl
remained, looking at the stars.

When Yeats's eyes adjusted to the deepening
dim, he realized she was crying. A sob drifted
with the scent of flowers. Yeats moved closer to
the cover of a tree several yards ahead, but when
he peeked out, the girl was coming right for him
along the main path.

He froze.

She was close enough to touch and dressed in a
thin lace tunic that swished as she walked. A shawl
covered her head. She must have heard him move,
for she stopped, then turned and peered into the
shadows. As she pushed back the branches, her
face was suddenly illuminated by moonlight.

Shaharazad!

"Khan?" she whispered.

Yeats gawked. "I . . . I . . ." The shawl had lifted

with the branches to show her hair flowing over her shoulders in thick black curls. She looked like a princess from a fairy tale.

"You're not Khan. What are you doing in there?" There was no alarm in her voice, only mild amusement.

"I . . . I . . ."

"Are you spying?"

"Uh . . ." He winced.

She stepped closer. "Listen to me, spy, because I warn you for your own good. Do you know what happened to the last spy that was found by Khan? And my father is even less merciful than Khan." She put her hands on her hips. "I am astonished that you eluded my pet. Still, I am happy for someone's company other than my nurse." She looked sideways at him. "Unless, of course, you are a thief. Be warned that I am armed." She pulled back the folds of her tunic to reveal a short knife.

"I am not a thief," Yeats managed. "But I am looking for something."

"And what might that be?" She folded her arms.

"You."

Her face brightened. "Did Mohassin send you? Oh deceitful, lovable cook! He cannot tell me himself but has sent his servant," she murmured. "Wait! I'm coming in!" Before he could reply, the girl parted the branches of his tree covering and stepped through.

She was so close their noses nearly touched. "There! Now, what does Mohassin have to say to me?"

Yeats tried to think. "Mohassin did not send me. I am here on my own."

"For what purpose?"

Taking a deep breath, Yeats ventured, "To help you, to save you from a danger. And to help my father."

She narrowed her eyes. "The poets have said, The face of an honest man hides nothing, while the face of a liar can be read by all."

She was almost as tall as Yeats, which surprised him since he was used to looking down at people his age. Her delicate curls and feminine clothes were deceiving, for when her arm brushed against his shoulder he felt the strength of an athlete, not a dainty royal.

"I am not a liar," he answered.

"Yet not telling all either. That is close to a lie. Tread carefully."

He swallowed. "I can't."

"Why?"

"Because you will think I am crazy."

She scrutinized him. "You are *not* witless. However, each man serves his own purpose. And what may yours be, I wonder?" She tugged him out of the tree branches into the moonlight. "What garments are these!" she exclaimed and touched his shirt. "You are from a distant land, I see. But I do not fear you. You have a trusting face. And familiar! Walk with me. My father allows no one but my maid to visit, and your company, deceitful or not, is welcome." She stopped after a few paces. "By all that is in heaven! I *have* seen you before. Swear it is so."

"You knew my father." Before she could query further he added, "And if everyone has their purpose I would very much like to know yours."

At the last second he remembered to add, "My lady." The stones crunched pleasantly beneath their feet and the moonlight opened a path before them. Yeats had the surreal sensation that the garden was a theater and the trees an audience. Blossoms fluttered down like butterfly ghosts and came to rest silently before their feet. Her next words broke his reverie.

"I want to know why the city weeps."

His stomach lurched. "You said that to Mohassin."

"So you *are* a spy!" she accused.

He shook his head. "No. But why do you need to know about the weeping? Do you really think you are Shaharazad?"

With the briefest smile she kept walking. "How intriguing! It is told that once there lived a man whose words were honey but whose garb was as slovenly as a boar. . . ."

"Is this a story?" Yeats interrupted.

Shaharazad nodded.

He sighed. "I was told you are familiar with all the stories and poets."

"I am. Shall I continue, stranger? And have you a name before I am interrupted again?"

"It is Yeats."

"Fascinating!" the girl exclaimed. "I know it not. Nor have I read it in any book. You are not from here."

"No. I am from another place." Peering suspiciously at the near bushes, Yeats whispered, "And neither are you. You just don't remember it."

Shaharazad tapped her lip. "I have read of this philosophy before. Does it not come from the eastern part of the empire?"

"It's not a philosophy. It's reality!" Yeats gestured in exasperation. "You don't belong here and you've got to come with me." He broke into a sweat. "Listen. I don't know why the city weeps. I'll find out! But, Shari, I've really come to find *you.*"

The girl frowned.

"Don't you know who you are?" Yeats pressed.

"I am the vizier's daughter."

"Yes, but who you *really* are? Don't you remember William Trafford?"

She stared ahead with half-closed eyes, as if

she was thinking hard. Her response, when it came, was deflating. "You are indeed strange, Yeats. Nonetheless, you are an answer to my prayers, for I have searched many days to find anyone who will tell me the mystery outside these walls. My father will not let me leave the palace, and his guards are sworn to execute anyone who speaks to me."

"Execute?"

A bell rang and Shaharazad gasped. "My father! Quickly now!" She grabbed his hand. The echo of many heavy footfalls sounded in the colonnade, followed by crunching stones. Spearheads glinted in the moonlight.

Shari pulled him across the lawn to the shelter of a torch-lit archway. They crouched against the wall as three servants carrying earthen jars passed. They could hear but not see the group of soldiers in the garden. Yeats looked at the girl closely. With her curls framing her cheeks she looked prettier than the picture in Gran's house.

"My chamber is through that door," she said. "Can you see it?"

He squinted through the archway into the palace. "Yes."

"I will wait for you tomorrow night."

"Tomorrow night?" Yeats exclaimed.

"Yes," the girl said. "Come at midnight when Rawiya, my maidservant, has left my chamber. There will be a diversion to distract the guards. Knock with a single rap. Find out the grief of the city and bring me news! Then I will reward you."

He panicked as the girl prepared to leave. "Wait! I just got here," he began.

She pressed something into his hands. "Here are the coins Mohassin refused. Go to the kitchens and find him. He will help with all your other needs. But you must go to him. There is no one else I trust. Take this ring. It is a sign for him that you are true. But do not tell him why you are here, for I must protect him too."

The voices from the garden faded. Shaharazad looked out briefly, then pulled him close. "There is a passage beyond the archway of the next colonnade. Follow it to its end. There you will find a door that can only be opened from the inside and so is not guarded at night. Follow the path to the main road. It will take you to the market and inns. In the morning, come back to the palace kitchens to find Mohassin." Shaharazad squeezed his hand. "I know you, though I know not from where. You warm my heart."

"Then come with me," he urged.

The flash of torchlight made them both look up. "Go, Yeats!"

She should be close to remembering! If only they had more time. "There is so much to explain," he said. "I need to tell you about my family, about my father, about Gran's library and where it all began. Can't you hide me somewhere so we can talk?"

"Unless you wish to spend the night in the garden hedge there is nowhere else," she said. "I am confined to the garden and my room. And how would I explain you to Rawiya, my maidservant? But tomorrow night I will send her on an errand. And I will create a distraction for the guards. At midnight. One knock on the door. Be ready! Now, go! Guards are coming."

There was nothing to be done. He could not

hide from bush to bush in the garden with guards tramping around all night. "Midnight, here!" he repeated. Cursing his luck, he rushed across the paving stones just as the guards came into full view. He shrank from the shadows cast by the spitting torches and hugged the wall. The girl gave a final wave, and Yeats was alone once more to face the Arabian night.

9

KHAN

When the guards left, Yeats headed in the direction of the passage Shari had described to him. A twig snapped behind him. He stopped breathing. What now? What else could be lurking that might be worse than guards? The gray trunks blurred as he swung around. He could hear the breath of a large creature. Seconds later something tickled the back of his neck.

A savage voice growled in his ear, "Why are you here?" Long whiskers trailed across his cheek and a powerful shoulder jostled him with ease. Two green eyes blinked.

It was a panther, black as pitch, whose eyes and glimmering teeth alone gave away its shape.

"Answer."

Yeats winced against the blast of its warm breath.

"I'm looking for someone," he stammered.

The giant cat sniffed; its wet nose greased Yeats's chin. Then it swung toward the sound of the retreating guards. Yeats stepped backward and the cat whipped a paw around his leg without turning. When its claws punctured his skin, Yeats screamed.

Suddenly he was on his back, the giant cat pressed against his chest, forcing all the air out of him.

"Another sound and I'll gouge your throat!"

"I won't," Yeats wheezed. "I promise." His leg throbbed: the weight of the cat was unbearable. Its teeth were dangerously close. "Please let me go."

"You prefer the company of the pirates?" mocked the panther. "Yes. I saw who brought you here. I would have tracked you faster but that foolish cook shut the inner gate on his way out."

The panther proceeded to wash a paw, bobbing its great claws in front of Yeats's nose.

"Are you going to kill me?"

The panther stopped and eyed the garden. "I cannot release you," it said simply. "For it is my position to guard those who live here. And you are an intruder."

"I didn't know this was your garden."

The cat continued licking itself, roughly scraping its claws across Yeats's shirt in the process. "This is not my garden." Its muscles tensed. It was going to bite his throat! Those horrible teeth ripping . . .

"I'm here for Shaharazad!" he cried desperately.

The green eyes flared. "Shaharazad?"

"Yes."

The panther extended a claw, pressing the point into Yeats's neck.

"Please don't kill me," he gasped. "I've got to bring that girl home."

The cat gave a low growl. "You've as much chance of that as of escaping my claws."

"Why?" Yeats asked breathlessly.

"She's under a spell. Surely your pirate friends told you."

Yeats gawked. "They did. How did you know?"

"Because," the giant cat said and rolled off his stomach, "I am a bookend."

Gasping, Yeats clutched his throat and sat up. The panther made no move to stop him.

"I happen to be searching for someone myself. A wish gone bad, you might say." The great creature sighed, a little sadly, Yeats thought, although he did not say so. "I work alone now and at double the effort. I envy your pirates that much."

Despite his fear Yeats couldn't help but appreciate the panther's beauty and mystique. "Who are you looking for?" he asked.

The panther's eyes gleamed. "A boy. His name is Roland. He entered this story a short time ago and remains lost in the town."

Yeats brightened. "My dad desperately needs Shaharazad to come home," he whispered. "If you let me go, we can help each other. I will do my best to look for Roland. I've got to go into the town tonight and I could use the company anyway. I could bring him back here."

The giant cat's tail thumped the garden floor. Yeats couldn't tell if it was angry or thinking. After a long pause it said, "All those within the confines of this book live and die accordingly. But you and I are not of this place. We smell its smells, breathe its air, and taste its food, but we know better, don't we? We know of the other place. It is indeed difficult to journey alone."

Yeats nodded. "I've only been here for an hour and already I'm homesick." He thought of the pirates abandoning him on the shore. "If you're a bookend, where is your partner?"

The big cat's tail thumped a little harder and Yeats wondered if he had pushed his luck too far. But the panther responded, "Lost to fire."

"I'm sorry," said Yeats.

"So am I," the animal said. "I will release you on one condition: that should you encounter Roland you must tell me. You will recognize him by his shaved head and black skin. I must find him quickly, for he has rightly and fairly broken the spell."

Yeats felt a rush of panic. "Why can't you find him? The pirates told me I would return to my world if I broke the spell."

The panther licked its paw ominously. "With my partner's untimely demise I work with only half the magic."

"I see. The pirates were separated for years, one in the library and one in the garden when Dad buried him. Does this happen to everyone? Do all wishes go bad?"

The panther snorted. "Rarely. With those two, I shouldn't wonder."

"I guess I'll have to take my chances," Yeats said. "Now, how will I reach you?"

The cat glanced over its shoulder. "Only at night do I stray from my mistress to search for the boy. Otherwise, I am here."

"Your mistress?"

"Shaharazad." The panther began to pace. "Go—if you will. But remember: Khan tracks you closely. If you should find Roland, do not dare to return to your world without first telling me. I have a duty while in this story to chew the legs of intruders. I do not let my quarry go easily. And I do not need the entanglements of another's wish."

The thump of Khan's great steps on the

ground was disconcerting, particularly so when the shimmering green eyes winked closed and Yeats lost sight of him.

"Khan?" Yeats whispered.

The cat was gone. Yeats scrambled to his feet and then dropped just as suddenly because of the pain in his leg. He touched it and his hands came up bloody. After further examination with his fingers, however, he determined the cat's scratches were not deep. They would mend soon enough. He gritted his teeth and tore a long strip from his shirt to bind the wound tightly. "Not a nice place so far," he told himself. "I've nearly been hung for hiding in a garden and killed by a panther!"

Yeats tested his leg, taking several steps toward the culvertlike passage Shaharazad had described. The grand conditions of the palace deteriorated rapidly the more he progressed. Brackish water leaked in rivulets from cracks in the wall, and the path became uneven. A little farther along, the torches stopped. He was in a rarely used part of the palace, and yet, he thought with a grin, it wouldn't surprise him if Shaharazad had been this way before. For someone who really wasn't who she thought she was, she certainly played the part well. In the few minutes he had known her he decided he liked her immensely.

He stared into the gloom, keeping one hand at the ready and the other feeling along the wall. He was plunged into the darkness. It never occurred to him that Shari could have deceived him. He knew there would be a door leading to the town.

Sure enough, within a minute the passage came to an abrupt end. Upon opening the door he was struck by a blast of dry heat, very different from the cool of the garden, even though he was still underground. A rocky path sloped away from the palace and wound its way to a cluster of tiny lights in the distance.

It was an awful feeling when he broke into the fresh air again. He crept like a sand crab along the dark and dusty track. Someone barked an order from high on the parapet, and Yeats pressed himself to the ground. Torchlight revealed a guard's silhouette on the sand. But the guard's back was turned and his hail was answered from the nearest tower. Yeats waited for the voices to stop before hurrying on.

He crossed a stream, stopping briefly to drink and wash the scratches on his leg. He wondered if this was part of the same river that met the sea near the palace. "Too small," he murmured. The world turned flat away from the walls of the palace, and the gray desert stretched to the horizon under the moon where it met the last crack of sunset.

Only a little heat came from the ground, the last vestige of a boiling day and cool night. He was glad to be wearing his running shoes. He wondered what his father and Shari had done for disguise and if their clothes were the very things that attracted attention and caused the girl to be taken. Then he frowned. "I'll have to find clothes somehow in the town," he said to himself. "Can't go around dressed like this. That'll bring guards in a hurry!"

Yeats wrapped his arms around his chest for warmth as he walked. Only the lamps, glowing from the town ahead, provided him with enough light to choose a direction. All else had turned to blackness. He stumbled frequently. To keep from falling he kept his eyes on the cluster of flat-roofed houses glinting like bone in the yellow lamplight.

"It's no good," he muttered. "I should have stayed with her. What if something happens to me out here and I can't get back?" The thought made him bite his lip. He imagined his parents sitting at the table in Gran's house, worrying to death about him. "Steady, Yeats," he murmured. "Dad got out. I will too. And I have information he didn't: I know how to break the spell and bring Shari back." He grimaced. "Theoretically."

Sometime later the ground surrounding the path became clearer. It happened so gradually that at first he did not realize there was a light shining from behind him. The brilliant moon traveled farther into the night sky, lighting the path to the town and the desert beyond. His footsteps crunched on the pebbly path.

Half an hour after setting out he came to his destination. There were walls here as well, surrounding the city, but nothing so ornate as at the palace. The gates were made of wood, weathered and beaten by the sun, and they stood wide open. More from neglect, he thought, then in welcome. There were no guards.

Through the gap the moonlight revealed whitewashed homes with cracked walls, most connected by flat-topped roofs. Lamplight flickered from a few arched windows, and Yeats smelled the acrid scent of oil burning. He turned at every sound: a cough, a baby's cry, his own scuffing feet. Something savage barked beyond the walls. There were scattered conversations as well, soft voices and whispers as families brought their day to a close.

And then something quite awful rose above the expected nocturnal noises. Weeping. There was no warning. It simply broke out in one home and spread to the rest. From every dwelling, grief swept the night air like a morbid wind.

"How horrible," he gasped. He covered his ears and ran between the homes. Shari was right; everyone was crying. What had happened to this place? The noise! He couldn't stand it.

Something ran across his path and he stopped.

He dropped to one knee. A scrawny cat rubbed against his legs. The sight of something familiar and friendly moved him to pick it up. He held it close, almost as a shield against the waves of grief still flowing from the homes.

"I bet you don't get a quarter of what Odysseus eats at Gran's," he whispered into its ear. The cat searched his hand. The thought of Gran's house made him suddenly weary. "I've got to lie down and rest somewhere," he told the cat. "The biggest day of my life is waiting tomorrow. I've got to rescue a vizier's daughter and save my family!"

A wail from the nearest window made him start. The cat finished licking his fingers and then jumped down from Yeats's arms. It walked to a doorway a few steps away. Yeats approached cautiously. A waft of fish smell hit him the moment he touched the door frame. Holding his nose, he stepped inside.

Wooden slab tables. A fish shop. Not the best place to sleep. Still, he reasoned, the awful smell might keep the curious away. It could be the perfect place to remain undetected till morning. And then he could think of another plan.

Lying on the floor was the worst option. He couldn't bear the idea of mice or rats running over his face. He climbed onto a table, then quickly jumped off. It was still damp. He searched around the spare room until he found a pile of empty onion sacks. He threw several on the table for a mattress and used another as a blanket. The business of readying himself for sleep renewed Yeats's confidence. He punched the sack that served as a pillow.

"They'll think I'm a beggar!" He grimaced. "And I suppose I am. I must wake before dawn and leave. I've also got to find some clothes. What does a boy wear here anyway?" He had not seen anyone his age other than Shaharazad, and he certainly did not want to look like her.

The cat jumped up and sat on his stomach. It did not appear to mind the fishy smell of the shop. Yeats stroked its back. So much had happened! He couldn't believe that only hours ago he was drinking tea in Gran's kitchen with his parents.

Now he was far from his family, lying on a stinking table with a cat as his only companion.

"Can't be helped," he murmured. "I'm here for a reason! The moment I get Shari back, and Mom sees her, there will be no doubt about what's happened. Mom will fall in love with Dad again. And who knows, maybe even old Mr. Sutcliff will get better when he sees his granddaughter."

A scuffling sound in the corner made him start. The cat whirled around to look as well. It was about to investigate when Yeats held out a restraining hand. "Wait. Stay here. It's only a rat or a mouse." He stroked the top of the cat's head until it settled back down.

Yeats pulled the onion sacks up higher on his chest. The wailing eventually stopped. The wildness of the day had exhausted him at last. His thoughts drifted. Shari was exactly as his father had described her. She was so determined. It was impossible to argue with her. The only thing that seemed to shake her confidence was how familiar he looked.

"I've got to make her remember," he said. He

took out the ring she had given him. When he leaned over to return the ring to his pocket, the necklace popped out from his shirt. The bell and marble jingled. He'd forgotten about the necklace. "Don't worry, Dad," he murmured. "It's kept me safe so far. I'll bring her back."

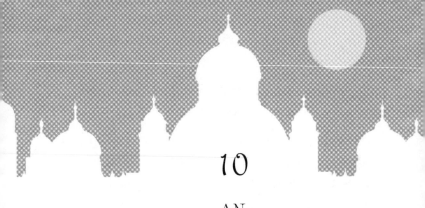

10

AN
EMPTY ROOM

When the sound of the wind from Yeats's departure reached upstairs, Mr. Sutcliff was the first to move. "The library! Quickly, now!" For an old man he managed the squawking stairs with amazing agility. The rest of the family followed him. They stopped at the glass doors to the library, now blown wide open.

"He's gone." Gran squeezed her eyes shut.

"Yeats!" Faith yelled. She pushed past her husband, calling up and down the stacks, "Yeats!"

"Over here." Mr. Sutcliff was standing between the shelves. There was a volume lying open on the floor at his feet. The mess of books and the open pages plainly told that someone had been there.

"He's gone then." Sutcliff nodded. "Good lad!"

"Gone?" Faith sputtered.

Mr. Sutcliff leaned down and examined two bookends. "Saints alive! There's two!" He nodded slowly and cast a glance around the room. "It starts to make sense now."

"What does?" Faith said, exasperated.

William lifted the book from the floor. "It's Collfield's."

"I knew it!" Gran clapped her hands. "Odysseus!" she called.

"Well, what are we going to do?!" Faith yelled, her voice choked by a sob.

William touched the pages. "There's nothing we can do. I can't remember how to get there!" He shook his head hopelessly. "What have I done? I shouldn't have come back here."

Mr. Sutcliff traced Skin's hat. The dust from the brim was strangely missing. Mr. Sutcliff stared long and hard at the book lying in William's hands. "No, William. You are wrong." He touched the treasure chest. "There is something we can do.

We have forgotten our stories. We have forgotten Aladdin and his lamp. We have forgotten the significance of wishes! And I am beginning to see at last how the pieces fit together." He glanced knowingly at the bookend. "Time for a little chat, my friend, isn't it?"

Faith murmured to Gran, "Perhaps Mr. Sutcliff should go to bed. He's talking to the bookend."

Gran rubbed her nose thoughtfully. "Heavens no, child! He's the only one who can help us."

11

CABBAGES
AND CLOTHES

G et out!"

Yeats sat bolt upright. An angry face, framed by a turban, bent near his. "Be gone, beggar's brat! You've had your ease. Clear out for those who make an honest living!"

Yeats fled, onion sacks scattering to the floor as he stumbled to the door.

Bleary-eyed, he gaped at the streets filled with merchants, stalls, and donkeys. Dust covered everything. He stumbled and caught himself in the doorway.

"Out!" came a final roar.

He leapt into the street, narrowly colliding with

a fish cart. Bulbous eyes stared up at him lifelessly from the stinking mass.

"Watch yourself, boy!"

"Just where are you from, dressed like that?"

"Keep moving!"

The only direction he could walk was straight ahead, upward toward the palace. At least the throbbing from his scratch had settled and his leg no longer hindered him. A strong scent of coffee, swiftly overtaken by the aroma of fresh bread, set Yeats's stomach grumbling. Three men on a mat took turns grinding beans in a pot. A steaming urn lay beside them. The men stared at him curiously. One of them pointed at his feet and called, "I'll give you a chicken for those sandals!" Yeats looked down at his running shoes. Then he was propelled forward along the street as someone shoved him in the back.

"I need a disguise," he muttered. From an alleyway just off the road he saw his chance. A string of laundry hung from twine between the homes. He darted into the alley, slinking along the wall and keeping a wary eye on the two windows above. There was a terrible smell and when he looked at the ground he saw fish bones and rotting cabbage leaves scattered everywhere.

The clothes were hung just out of reach between the two windows. He felt a twinge of guilt. It wasn't right to steal, and even more so from people who had so little. But what else could he do?

Yeats jumped at a tunic clipped to the middle of the line that hung a little lower then the rest. His fingers skimmed the hem. He tried again and managed to grip the cloth with his thumb and finger for a split second. On his third try the garment came free and Yeats fell to the ground in triumph with the tunic on his head.

As he was dusting himself off it dawned on him that he was going to have to remove his own clothes in order to put on the stolen tunic. "That's all right," he murmured. "I'll leave mine here. That way, it's not stealing. It's trading." He was down to his underwear and running shoes when he heard a giggle. He grasped the tunic to his chest and tried to cover himself. From the window on the other side of the alley a head peered down. It was a girl, somewhat younger than him.

Yeats did not know what to say. He glanced at the tunic in his hands. "Sorry," he whispered. "But I've left my own clothes here to replace it."

There was another giggle and the girl said softly, "It belongs to Vignan. He lives next to us. He pulls my hair. I won't tell." She leaned out a little farther and he saw her eyes and cheerful face.

"Thank you," said Yeats. He struggled into the tunic. Then he hastily folded the remaining coins into the waistline of his underwear. The running shoes he left propped against a wall.

"Are you hungry?" the girl whispered.

"Yes, I am."

She disappeared for a moment and Yeats wondered if he should leave. Just as he was about to go the girl returned. "We don't have much," she said. "But you can have my breakfast. Catch?"

Yeats held up his hands and caught a half cabbage. "Thank you!"

"You should go," the girl said. "My mother is coming."

"I think you are a wonderful person," he answered. "If Vignan pulls your hair again, tell me, and I'll punch him in the nose."

The girl covered her mouth in a burst of giggles and disappeared from the window. Yeats made for the street.

He merged into the traffic with precision this time, slipping in between two carts. The ground was hard packed and he cried out when he stepped on a sharp stone. "I should have kept the shoes!" he muttered.

Despite the discomfort of walking barefoot, he was quickly distracted by the amazing sights and sounds around him. There was so much happening he didn't know where to look first. No wonder his father and Shari had wished for an adventure like this. Everything was so vivid and real. And the smells! Both good and bad mingled in a profusion of scents. Baked bread and fruit, animal manure, and sweat from many people overwhelmed his senses. While he walked he munched on his cabbage. The bitter leaves made him long for hot buttered toast and honey.

A man a few strides ahead suddenly veered off the main road. He raised his robe and urinated. Dust rose over the gathering puddle. A beggar, missing both eyes, raucously gathered a wad of saliva in his mouth and spat amid the sandals of the nearest people. No one even acknowledged it. Everyone was carrying something and trying to get somewhere faster than everyone else.

There was drudgery in the faces of the people, reflecting a mood that reminded Yeats of his father. The people lifted their feet like those with burdens too heavy to bear. "It's a hard life," Yeats murmured. "And no wonder, when the king of the country is murdering their daughters!"

No sooner had the words left his mouth when a terrible wail made him choke on his cabbage. A row of black-clad women came into view, their robes covered in dust. They sat on the ground scooping the dirt with their hands and throwing it into the air.

They were sitting near an unfinished wall made of smooth flat stones. Each stone was splashed with whitewash and placed on the next.

As Yeats watched, the veiled women raised their arms to greet an approaching figure. It was a woman wrapped in black with only her eyes exposed. She walked alone, stopping every few feet to allow her tears to splash onto the stone she carried. Her grief was painful to watch. The wailing reached a crescendo when the woman stooped to place her stone on the wall.

"There must be hundreds of stones," Yeats murmured. "Perhaps even a thousand!" He sucked in a breath when he realized the terrible truth. Each stone represented a dead girl! He squeezed his eyes to shut out the scene. The noises he had heard the previous night were mothers and fathers weeping for their daughters. Now he had an answer to Shari's question. Oh, why had she wished to travel into such a tragedy?

He forced himself to look. The woman had joined the others on the ground, throwing fistfuls of dust into the air to show her grief. The injustice of the scene strengthened his resolve. He scowled fiercely. It was time to find Shaharazad. "Don't worry, Mom," he whispered. "I'm coming back.

I *will* make it back!" He looked up and angrily brushed a tear away. "And I'm bringing Shari with me! This ends tonight!"

"Get on!" a voice boomed, and someone pressed a basket of fruit against his shoulders.

Yeats spun around and raised his fist. He stared into the startled eyes of a farmer. The man warily moved around him. Yeats rubbed his temples. "What am I saying? The poor guy has probably lost a daughter. Sorry!" he called too late for the man to hear him.

The sun broke over the eastern horizon, illuminating the palace domes standing boldly against the morning sky beyond the town. It did not look as far away as his nocturnal journey had suggested. Somewhere in that maze was a girl, the key to his family's problems.

His stomach growled. The cabbage was a start but not enough. Working through the crowd, he found a fruit seller's stand readied for the day's business.

The street was not like any market Yeats had seen before. Various-size baskets and sacks lay uncovered on the ground and clustered around the merchants. Interspersed with pomegranates, lemons, and melons were nuts and seeds. Yeats gazed uncertainly. The merchant was engaged with a customer who was bargaining for a melon. Beside the largest basket another boy stood idly staring at the street. While the merchant was talking, the boy glanced at Yeats, smiled, and stole a pomegranate. He disappeared into the crowd.

Yeats picked up a dried fig. The other fruit looked like it might require a knife. The merchant addressed him warily and Yeats fumbled for a coin. He wasn't good at this sort of thing—he was better at words than at math. But one of the coins felt heavier than the others.

"How many?" the merchant queried.

Yeats showed the coin. "Ah . . . four?"

"What else will you have?"

Yeats stared blankly.

The merchant's lip twisted into a cunning smile. He looked Yeats up and down, his gaze lingering on his fair hair and turbanless head. "No need! Take the four figs and go in peace."

"Wait," Yeats fumbled at his waist. "I've got other coins. What about this one?"

No longer smiling, the merchant pressed forward. "Who are you? I have not seen you before. And where did you get such money? Have you stolen it?" His voice brought scowls in Yeats's direction.

"No! Of course not." He felt a prickle of sweat behind his ear.

"Who are you?" a woman asked.

"I . . . I'll just take the figs!" Yeats grabbed his fruit, tossed a coin at the merchant, and then ran toward the gates.

Shouts erupted. "A thief! A thief!" Several people leapt out of Yeats's way. He made for the thick of the crowd and disappeared into the mass of jostling merchants. He looked back after a few minutes and it appeared that no one was chasing him.

Outside the main town the long line of farmers and merchants thinned, and Yeats slowed to catch his breath and chew on a fig. In the distance, the palace rose up majestically from the desert, far enough to give him time to think. The figs were a welcome relief from the bitter cabbage. The dust was thick and already Vignan's freshly cleaned tunic was turning the color of the red earth. He thought again of the friendly girl who had helped him in the alley. If only there was someone like her ahead!

He joined a procession of carts and people carrying baskets toward the palace. A donkey brayed and a moment later Yeats had to step over a steaming pile of manure.

The crowd grew thicker closer to the palace gates. He caught his breath against a wall. He munched on another fig and spat the stem at the feet of the moving crowd.

"Stupid!" he chided himself. Some rescuer! He couldn't even buy fruit without drawing attention.

The crowd pressed forward through the enormous gate to the palace. Hewn slabs formed the archway and, open on either side, tall timbers made an impressive door. In the daylight, the roadways and walls gleamed white and channeled the people under a myriad of branches.

He had to find Mohassin. But where were the kitchens? He stood uncertainly at a fork in the great road while people brushed by.

He was about to merge into the crowd when suddenly someone yelled, "You'll catch trouble for it, Ali, if those cabbages are not on the King's table by midday."

A tall young man pushed a cart full of cabbages along the right-hand road. Yeats hurried after him. The road was so packed that Yeats had to jump up above the crowd occasionally to follow the cabbage seller's bobbing turban. It all looked so different in the daylight; he saw nothing of the route he had taken the previous evening. Somewhere ahead was the door that led to Shaharazad's chamber. If he could just find Mohassin! His only chance was to follow the cabbage seller and hope that he was headed in the right direction.

Yeats made use of his size to push through the crowd. He stopped saying "Excuse me" after he realized that everyone else was pushing too, the shorter people more than anyone. For one brief moment he lost sight of his quarry. He stood up on a cage full of colorful birds and looked. The cabbage seller had stopped under the shadow of an arched entryway.

"Get off!" shouted a voice below.

"Sorry!" called Yeats and he jumped back into the crowd. He sidled up to Ali and his cart. The seller was desperately defending himself to an angry cook.

"The roads are madness today. Look at them!"

The cook waved a finger. "They are no less mad than yesterday or a thousand days before that! Watch yourself, Ali. Or I may get my cabbages from another. Is there such darkness in your heart that you would keep his lordship waiting for his meal?"

Another figure appeared behind the cook. "What is all this talk of darkness on such a fine morning?"

Mohassin! Although he was now dressed in an apron, Yeats recognized him immediately. Yeats took the ring from his pocket and clasped it tightly.

"Look at poor Ali," Mohassin continued. "You have turned his face as white as his turban. And over cabbages! Go heat the fires. I will take the cabbages."

Ali bowed low, then hurriedly unloaded his vegetables into giant baskets on the floor. Yeats remained frozen to the wall. He had to speak to Mohassin. But would he listen?

"Filth!" croaked a voice at his knees. Yeats recoiled from a mangled figure he had mistaken for a heap of onion sacks. A beggar, lying on the ground, with a crumpled face that looked as worn as the cloak he was wearing, stared him down. "My spot, young maggot. Mohassin! Tell this maggot to leave my spot!"

Yeats held his ground and his breath as well.

Mohassin came closer and stared curiously at Yeats. He was not as old as Yeats had first thought, at least, not quite as old as Mr. Sutcliff. But years of hard work and sun had taken their toll, judging by his bent back and weathered face. He wiped his sweating forehead with a cloth.

"God's blessings, child," he said. "Do not mind Mustafa's scolding. The cabbages from my kitchen doors feed the rich and poor alike."

Yeats nodded weakly. He couldn't find his voice.

"Come, child. There is enough. No, Mustafa! Do not shake your stick! Eat your cabbage stew with thankfulness or I'll put you around the corner."

The beggar was mortified and tried to make amends. "Nice maggot. Come and sit with Mustafa. There is room!"

Still unable to speak, Yeats opened his hand to reveal Shaharazad's ring. The effect was immediate. The beggar pointed in astonishment and opened his mouth.

Mohassin pounced. He clapped a hand over the begger's mouth and hissed, "Have you not always eaten your fill here?"

The beggar nodded.

"Then fear not and speak not."

Before Yeats could retract his prize, Mohassin pulled him into the palace kitchens. Fires from two stone hearths, one at either end of the large room, filled the space with heat and flickering light. No wonder Mohassin was sweating! Earthen pots, herbs, and plants hung from lattices above their heads. The air was filled with spice. Two cooks laboring over a pot looked up at him.

"Young fool!" Mohassin whispered. "Why endanger the lady? Put the ring away!" He whisked Yeats into a storeroom shelved floor to ceiling with baskets. The odor of rotten cabbage was nauseating. "Speak quickly," Mohassin whispered. "We've already been noticed."

Yeats lifted the ring again hopefully.

Mohassin released him. Then he folded his hands in prayer. "I know the lady's token. Give it to me. There now, why are you here? What does she require and how have you managed to see her?"

Yeats shook his head, unsure of where to start. "I can't tell you! She told me not to. But she said you would help me."

Mohassin's shrewd gaze held him firmly. "I must honor her wishes, of course. Unless it presents a danger to herself. What is it you need?"

Yeats looked up sharply. "Take me to her chamber at midnight."

Twirling the end of his beard thoughtfully, the

man answered, "A most unusual request. Highly unusual."

"It is very important," Yeats said. "And I need your help. I don't know how to get to there from here. I can't remember the way. But I must be there by midnight because that is when she . . . she will be expecting me."

Mohassin rested his hands on his portly belly. "How in the realm of heaven did you manage to meet her in the first place? The palace is sealed off from the town and the garden is guarded by more than just palace soldiers."

"I . . . I was taken there. By people who know my father." It was partially true. Mohassin was unconvinced.

"And what, pray, is your father's name?"

"William Butler Trafford."

"He is a merchant? Certainly not royalty—not from the way you are dressed. And a foreigner."

Yeats peered down at his robe. "These aren't my regular clothes!"

The old man raised his eyebrows. "I should hope not."

"Will you help me?"

Mohassin regarded him thoughtfully. Finally he chuckled. "Shaharazad is always up to some new mischief. I imagine she is hungry for young company—strange as it appears to my eyes. And you are but a child! No harm to it, I think." He turned the ring over in his hand. "Although it is a dangerous game you two are playing. If you are caught, your head will hang from the palace gates."

Yeats held himself steady against the wall. He tried to hear Mohassin's next words but there was the image of his own head hanging. . . .

"You will need servant's clothes," Mohassin was saying. "I will garb you as a cook's assistant. If you are met on the way, you shall say you are delivering a sleeping draft to ease her ladyship's dreams."

Despite his assistance, Yeats sensed mistrust in the old man's words. He returned the cook's steady gaze as a show of good faith. Yeats had to gain his trust. It was his only hope of getting to Shaharazad.

The sound of wailing women rose above the clamor of the crowds. A wave of pain crossed Mohassin's face. "*That* is something Shaharazad need not know about." He gripped Yeats firmly. "You know that, don't you—foreigner though you be? She must not learn of what is happening."

Yeats shook loose. "I'm here for something else!"

The old man scowled. "Who are you, child?"

"Mohassin!" a gruff voice interrupted. A man holding a curved sword stood in the doorway. His robes were black and a silk scarf covered his mouth and nose. His silver helmet had a spike at the top. "Trouble?"

Palace guard! It was Yeats's first good look at one and the sight was enough to make him wish he never saw another. The guard's bare arms rippled with muscles and there was a scar on his face that ran from the corner of one eye to his chin.

Straightening, Mohassin turned. "No. Not yet. The new assistant doesn't seem to know the difference between a cabbage and an onion."

The guard laughed cruelly. Then he ran his

finger along the flat side of his blade. "Shall I give him a lesson?"

Mohassin studied Yeats thoughtfully, as if waiting to see his reaction. "No, thank you," he said finally. "The assistant will need both his hands, and all his fingers too. But you will return to check his progress?"

Yeats thrust his hands behind his back.

"With pleasure." The guard left the doorway for the busy street.

"Shaharazad asked me to help her," Yeats blurted before the old cook could speak. "She did! Honestly! I swear I'm telling the truth."

Mohassin grunted. "Since her ladyship was a baby I have brought food to her table. I was the cook when her mother was a child! Never before has such dread fallen upon her ladyship's family and this town. I have sworn no harm will come to her." He gripped Yeats's arm tightly. "Do you understand? You will find little mercy from me if I discover you are lying." The cook gave a frightening glare. "It must be my lady's swordsmanship."

When Yeats did not respond, Mohassin added,

"She practices her swordsmanship at night. In secret. I assume you will be her sparring partner. Her own servant, Rawiya, is not trained in such arts." He looked Yeats up and down. "I can't believe you've even held a sword! And where she found you . . ." He sighed and then released Yeats. "In the meantime you must learn to be inconspicuous. I will show you your work for the day." He lowered his voice. "And I will show you the way by which you must enter the palace tonight. Provided," he added ominously, "you are found to be trustworthy. If not, I shall call for the guard."

All Yeats could do was nod. In only a few minutes he had been threatened with losing both his head and his hands. From the short time he had spent in this land, he did not doubt it was going to be a challenge to stay in one piece.

12

THE
COOK'S ASSISTANT

Yeats tied on an apron and hurried to catch up to Mohassin.

"The fire must be kept burning," the old cook instructed. "When you are not chopping onions or peeling garlic you will check the fire regularly." Yeats noticed an enormous pot in the center of the room with live coals beneath it. Steam poured out of the top and he could just make out something murky and brown boiling slowly and making frothy bubbles. Several featherless birds hung from a hook above the pot. Their heads were missing. Yeats shivered.

As they carried on into the next room, Mohassin continued to give instructions and pointed at

various plants or herbs. Occasionally he shouted orders to servants who were all busy at work, most of them chopping cabbages or onions. The heat was oppressive.

"My soups and sauces are used by all the royalty," Mohassin commented. "Although my humble kitchen is outside the palace, I have many customers within it. So you will make certain that every chop, every leaf, every seed of cumin is to its exact measure." Yeats nodded at everything the cook said but desperately hoped he would not be asked to repeat any of it.

When the tour ended Yeats was left alone to manage the fire. While he stirred the coals his mind raced with everything that had happened. At least he was headed in the right direction now and not lost in a strange town. He was back on track; he had found Mohassin, he was near the palace, and if all went well he would see Shaharazad that very night.

Yeats blew gently at the base of the fire and a great flame leapt up. There was movement near his knees, and when he looked down he saw a crowd of nasty-looking bugs scurrying from the circle of rocks around the fire. He stood up quickly with a gasp and the bugs shot across the floor to hide under a basket of cabbages.

"I don't think this place would pass health inspection," Yeats muttered.

Nearby, his fellow servants glanced at him periodically. One or two gave him encouraging looks and an older man showed Yeats how to control the flame when the coals died down.

Once he understood his chores, Yeats returned to his thinking. It was not clear if Mohassin trusted him or not. Every time the old cook checked up on him (which felt like every few minutes), there was a hint of distrust in his voice and his eyes. Shari's ring had done the trick so far, but would Mohassin truly take him to see the girl at midnight? Or would there be a guard waiting for him in the darkness instead? And what did Mohassin mean about the girl practicing swordsmanship? She had not said anything about that. He thought of her determined eyes and nodded to himself. Yes, she was definitely someone who would know how to use a sword. That might make things more difficult.

He was still mulling over his thoughts when the old cook reappeared with a small platter and cup in his hands.

"Come and sit here, boy. Eat and listen to your next duties," he said in an overly loud voice. The platter contained a lump of sweaty cheese and a piece of flat bread. Yeats gulped it down without a moment's thought. The cup contained a yellow liquid. Yeats could not stop his face from scrunching at the taste.

"What is wrong?" Mohassin queried. "It is good wine." Yeats raised his eyebrows. He suddenly thought of his father, scrunching his face after drinking the Scotch in Gran's kitchen. Yeats clenched his fist.

And then the cook said something to lift Yeats's spirits. Holding a cabbage in one hand and a knife in the other, Mohassin proceeded to describe the proper method of cutting the vegetable. In between his loud instructions the old cook inserted hurried, whispered directions. "You will accompany me into the palace for the noon meal. I will bring you to the inner pool and point to the hall where you may find my lady's chamber. You will have to keep a sharp memory of everything, as the palace is not as easy to navigate at night. I assume you know my lady's door?"

"Yes," Yeats answered. The cook nodded almost imperceptibly and then held the cabbage up into the light of an open doorway.

"Should you cut too deeply on the first stroke you can always salvage the cabbage by turning it over and making a second here, like so," Mohassin said.

It was all cabbages and onions until lunchtime. The smoke made him choke and the onions made his eyes burn so badly that Yeats found himself longing for the afternoon adventure to begin.

Mohassin returned, carrying a steaming pot in either hand. "Take these," he commanded. "I will buy bread in the market and then we will go to the palace." As they left for the palace, Mustafa, the beggar, gave a start as they stepped out the doorway. He reached out with his crutch and cackled with laughter when Yeats stumbled. Yeats regained his balance and gave Mustafa his best frown. The beggar cupped his hands around his mouth and said, "Maggot!" Mohassin, several strides ahead, did not notice and advanced toward a bread stall.

Once the bread was purchased Mohassin kept Yeats close as they worked their way through the crowd. With every step the old cook plied him with questions.

"Tell me about your father and these people he knows who have managed a private audience with my lady."

Yeats swallowed. This was dangerous ground. How could he describe Skin and Bones without raising Mohassin's suspicions? He decided it was best to talk about his father. He chose his words carefully, thinking of the language he heard around the university back home.

"My father is a scholar," Yeats began. "A learned man. When he was here . . . some time ago . . ." Yeats could feel his cheeks flushing as he fumbled for words. "He helped Shari . . .

Shaharazad." Ahead of them, the carts stopped and people were yelling.

Mohassin nodded. "It is common for palace people to hire foreign tutors. But I have not heard of your father before."

"Yes," said Yeats eagerly. "We are from very far away. You would not have heard of him."

"And my lady's father?" Mohassin continued. "He has brought you here?"

"Not exactly. These people my father knows . . ." They reached the carts, and Mohassin motioned for Yeats to stop speaking. Yeats breathed a sigh of relief and silently scolded himself for bringing up the pirates again. One thing was certain: Mohassin was shrewd. The best plan of action was to avoid his questions whenever possible.

A cow lay on the road and the carts were forced to stop.

"Come," said Mohassin. "The beast might be there all day. And we have business at the palace." The cook led Yeats around the milling crowd of farmers and merchants and then rejoined the path a little farther along. The distraction created by the cow brought a little relief for Yeats, as Mohassin did not raise the topic of the pirates again. Instead, he grew more agitated as they walked and told Yeats of various passages and rooms to avoid once they were inside.

"I cannot help you tonight," Mohassin said. "God help you if you are caught, for I will deny that I ever met you." He spoke so matter-of-factly that Yeats was left feeling a little cold inside. He had not forgotten that his father had almost lost his head in this place.

"This way!" said Mohassin. Yeats looked up. The palace loomed large above them, and Yeats was startled again by the magnificence of the high walls and the flowing script engraved into the stone. There were guards everywhere and the sun glistened off their pointed helmets.

There was a servants' door some distance away from the main gates and it was to this entrance that Mohassin hastened. "Keep your head down," he said. "The less you are seen now the more secure your disguise tonight." He raised an eyebrow and looked thoughtfully at Yeats. "Although it may serve our purposes better if tonight you are a maidservant."

"But I'm not a girl," Yeats protested.

The cook smiled. "Perhaps you will be this evening." They said no more as they approached the entrance. A guard opened the servants' door. He recognized Mohassin and he motioned them in.

Yeats gasped. Daylight streamed into a courtyard with an elaborately tiled floor in the form of a rampaging bull. The eyes of the beast were bright red and so vividly angry that Yeats stepped cautiously to avoid its giant head. Airy curtains drifted above them like ghostly arms. Plants and shrubs surrounded a pool and fountain at the far end of the courtyard. Servants passed to and fro carrying platters, jars, clothes, and parchments. Yeats twitched his nose. He smelled coffee again, and bread. His stomach rumbled.

"Look there!" whispered Mohassin, and he nodded to the right of the pool. He leaned closer to Yeats. "That is the way to the lady's chamber. Do you see it? There is a garden there as well."

A long hallway branched away through a set of open doors. Yeats nodded. The cook continued. "Our way continues on. We cannot go there now. You will need to find the pool to set yourself right. If you become lost, always find the pool. It is the largest in the palace and the hallways lead back to it. At night, there are torches set around it to illuminate the surface."

Yeats nodded. The pool would be hard to miss. Mohassin led them off to the left, to the one doorway that looked darker than the other light-filled adjoining chambers. Passing through the gloom Yeats saw a smoky, high-ceilinged room, five times the size of Mohassin's kitchen. Servants were bustling in and out with platters of bread, cheese, and vegetables.

"More salt!" someone shouted.

"Bread is ready!" shouted another. A servant pushed past Yeats and said, "His Highness Prince Vikram has stomach pains and does not want his rice cakes!"

"Bring it here," someone called. "We know what to do with it!" There was an outburst of laughter.

"I'll take his wine," said another.

"You take everyone's wine," came the retort. There was more laughter.

At that moment a bustling figure came through the doorway. "I'll give you all something to think about if you're not busy!" The officious man carried a stick, which he smacked into his open palm. The servants fell quiet and picked up their pace.

"How many people are in this place?" Yeats whispered in wonder.

"In the palace?" countered Mohassin. "Hundreds of royalty. But not nearly so many as there are servants. Enough, now. No more speaking."

They stayed only long enough for Mohassin to deliver the pots of soup. "Lay them down there," he directed. Yeats set them down in front of a thin, nervous-looking man with an enormous white turban. The man gave Yeats a doleful stare.

As they moved away, Mohassin remarked, "He is one of the royal tasters. It is his honor to find poison in the food and to die in the stead of a prince or princess." Yeats glanced back. The taster lifted the lid off one of the pots and sniffed. Then he slowly dipped a spoon into the soup.

"What happens if he finds poison?" Mohassin said, anticipating Yeats's question. "Once he is dead, guards are sent to find the cook who made the soup. This can be difficult sometimes because many servants are involved in making and preparing the food." He sighed. "There have been entire kitchens beheaded."

Yeats gulped.

Mohassin waved a hand. "Tasters should not complain. At least they taste the best food in the land. All day long. What a glorious manner in which to die!" He spoke the words wistfully. Yeats thought of Mohassin's kitchen, his cabbages and soups, and the piles of vegetables pouring into the pantry. The man was clearly dedicated to cooking. Yeats could see why Shaharazad and the royals trusted him. It was uncomfortable to think that the old cook did not trust Yeats, and he wondered if he should simply try to tell the whole truth. But how could anyone be expected to believe it? That was a disturbing thought, considering that he had come here with the purpose of convincing Shari of the same thing.

When they came back into the light of the hallway, Yeats took a moment to get his bearings. The pool gleamed pleasantly and ahead of him he could see the raging bull mosaic. Mohassin watched him closely.

"Do not trust the bull," he said. "There is a bull mosaic at every entrance. Only the pool is a trustworthy guide. There are many smaller pools in the royal gardens. But this is the only one inside."

The walk back to the town was uneventful other than that Mohassin appeared to grow more agitated with each step. He glanced at Yeats frequently and was on the verge of saying something many times, but he held his tongue. Finally, as they neared the town gate, Mohassin said, "Tell me again how you managed to get so close to her ladyship without the guards being alerted."

As they moved through the milling crowds Yeats had to yell. "My father's friends took me there!"

He winced at the thought of the pirates being *friends* of his father. That was certainly stretching the truth. Mohassin caught the look on his face.

"Who are these *friends*?"

Yeats sidestepped a cart and then moved back closer to Mohassin. "They come from the same place I do, and they know Shaharazad too."

Mohassin led them to the kitchen entrance where Ali had brought the cabbages. Mustafa was napping against the wall and did not wake as they passed him.

"Are they royalty?" Mohassin asked.

"No."

"Soldiers?"

They were standing in the pantry, and Yeats was feeling more claustrophobic with every question. For a cook, Mohassin sure knew how to ask pointed questions. "Not exactly," Yeats answered.

Mohassin's voice was growing hostile. "Mercenaries? Spies?"

Yeats felt a little dizzy from the questions and the potency of moldy vegetables in the enclosed space. "Well, no. I mean, I don't think you could call a pirate . . ." Too late, the word slipped out and Mohassin pounced.

"Aha! A pirate!"

"No!" Yeats tried to recover. "They are not like regular pirates."

"Why are you working for pirates? Who is paying you?" Mohassin demanded.

Paying him? No one was paying him. Unless . . . "Shaharazad!"

"Show me!" Mohassin commanded.

Yeats fumbled for the coins. Mohassin's eyes widened as the coins appeared.

"Silver! These were the coins offered to me! You were spying! What have you done to her! Have you harmed her, you young snake? And where are your pirates? Does someone call for her blood as one of the last young women left in the city? Her ladyship is in danger!"

Yeats pushed back against the cabbage and onion baskets. "I swear to you I mean her no harm!"

But the cook's suspicion could not be assuaged.

"Guard!" Mohassin yelled and threw out his arms to prevent an escape.

"You were supposed to help me!" Yeats pleaded. "Remember the ring? She said you would help me. Where's your loyalty?"

"I will not help an enemy of Shaharazad!" There was movement behind Mohassin. Another cook entered and brandished a wooden spoon. Behind him stood a guard, the same one from the morning. His sword glinted in the light streaming from the doorway.

"We have a traitor in our midst!" Mohassin pointed.

"I'm not a traitor," Yeats said. "You must believe me. I've come a long way to save her. I'm on her side." He clambered onto the baskets, squishing vegetables as he went.

"Come here, little traitor," the guard cooed. "I will make your end swift enough. Your head will join the cabbages!"

"Ah ha ha ha!" cackled Mustafa from the doorway. "Cabbage head! Cabbage head!"

Reaching the shelves, Yeats climbed for the

ceiling. The guard pushed ahead of the cooks and slashed. A spray of wood splinters splashed over his knuckles.

"Are you crazy?" Yeats shouted. "I'm just a kid!" He kicked at the guard's helmet and sent a basket of onions cascading to the floor. The men leapt aside, and Yeats suddenly had an idea.

He began hurling onions. The cook dropped his spoon with a cry of pain when an onion caught him on the nose. Yeats shouted triumphantly. When the onions ran out he threw fist-size garlic bulbs. Mohassin yelped.

"Treacherous filth," the guard growled.

"More!" shouted Mustafa. "More!"

In a moment, all three men were hurling onions. Mohassin's turban had begun to unwind and trailed in front of his eyes. He threw with a fury. A large onion caught Yeats on the cheek. In addition to the sting, he lost his balance and the entire shelf wobbled precariously. The room swirled in front of him and the men gaped with open mouths.

"Look out!" the cook screamed.

Too late, the shelf toppled with Yeats riding its crest. There was a terrible crash. Cabbages and onions bounced out the doorway. Between his feet the point of a scimitar stuck up through the head of a cabbage. The guard groaned.

"Oooooh!" said Mustafa and clapped his hands. "Clever maggot."

Yeats pushed off from the pile and fled into the busy street.

13

A GARDEN
AND A PRISON

Since dawn Shaharazad had idled in the garden, waiting for midnight under the watchful eye of her maidservant, Rawiya. There was little the old woman missed, and Shaharazad had done her best to appear eager for pampering. Rawiya had spent her life tending to children from the royal court and there was nothing she felt more comfortable doing. If Rawiya suspected that Shaharazad was waiting for a visitor that very night all would be lost. And so Shaharazad pouted and complained as was her right as the daughter of the royal vizier, all the while feeling sick with anticipation. White blossoms covered the grounds, and she busied herself with twining the new petals into a coronet. Her gaze flickered often to the trees.

At her feet, Khan was restless, incessantly stirring from the shade and rubbing his back against her legs. He, too, was interested in the garden shadows.

At the fountain's edge three minstrels played, one of them singing. It was the vizier's command that music should blanket the sounds from the town outside.

Shaharazad sighed. "Ah, Rawiya! Such a glorious day. My father, the vizier, long may he guide us, has promised to fit me with the finest gown from the bazaar! And within this very hour! I am shaking!"

"Indeed, he has, my lady." Rawiya poured her a cup of cool wine. "But let my lady also remember that the vizier is the busiest of men in the kingdom. At any hour of the day or night, the King, long may he reign, might require your father's infinite wisdom on this matter or that."

Shaharazad pouted. "Surely not on the day he has promised his daughter the finest dress in the kingdom!" She brushed aside the wine.

Pleased, Rawiya wiped the rim of the cup, then offered it again. "Is it not said, 'Happy is the maiden whose patience grants her the favor of the gods?'"

Shaharazad turned briefly to hide her smile. This time she took a sip. "Perhaps you are right. I fear then he is delayed and the dress shall not come before the markets close."

"Come, sweet Shaharazad. Be comforted. Recite words of the poets and fill the air with sweeter sounds than these musicians."

The singer scowled but did not lower his voice, for his life depended on it.

"Posture, my lady!" Rawiya reminded, and Shaharazad sat up straighter.

Perhaps Rawiya was right, she thought. Poetry or a story would pass the time more swiftly. Her heart leapt at the prospect of her evening plans. She closed her eyes and took a deep breath. "All right. A story then, from a far-off land, about a brave girl and a terrible Sultan. I warn you, the translation will not be perfect, but I will do my best." She allowed the words and images to form and then began:

"In the time of kings and sons of kings there ruled a cruel lord.

He gathered all the mighty men from hill and vale and fjord.

Upon the warriors gathered there the Sultan laid this quest:

'To win my lovely daughter's hand, thou must be the best.'

So fair she was, in wisdom sound

Her words fell not onto the ground

But captured all who listen well

Upon their ears, a beauty spell."

Rawiya raised an eyebrow. "Would I know this maid, my lady? She seems familiar."

"Shhhh," Shaharazad whispered.

Rawiya motioned to a servant. "Bring a fan! It is hot even in the shade. And pomegranate juice. Posture, my lady."

"By the gods, Rawiya, you interrupt."

"My lady. I beg you, continue."

Shaharazad smiled. If midnight was slow in coming, the least she could do was entertain.

"A tournament was readied there,

The grounds enriched with garlands fair.
And lords and ladies far and wide,
Came hither to the Sultan's side.
In cloistered room his daughter wept
Privy to the taxes that he kept.
Could not but hear the groans of misery,
Her people's yoke of usury.
The Sultan's heart was black as oil,
And fainted not at the people's toil."

Rawiya glanced toward the palace nervously. "Must you choose stories with bad rulers and unhappy people?" Apparently the musicians were listening as well, for they began playing even louder.

Shaharazad, however, was lost in the telling and failed to see the servants' consternation. She focused beyond Rawiya, as if an audience of greater proportion sat in the sunlight.

"The Sultan's daughter made her choice,
Stood resolute and raised her voice:
'Let the evil of this land stop with me,
And by my life! I'll set them free!'"

"Oh, help us all!" Rawiya clasped her hand to her mouth. "My lady! You must stop now!"

The girl stirred, blinked, and disengaged from her audience. "But this is where the Sultan's daughter . . ."

Rawiya clapped her hands and bade the other servants to do likewise. "All of you, quickly now! Let us go to the inner pool. We must get away from this oppressive heat." Shaharazad sighed resignedly, rose, and followed her maidservant inside. But not before she cast one last, long look at the shadows of the garden.

Meanwhile, Yeats ran for his life. He shouldered through the crowds and into the narrow alleys, hunting for a hiding place. Yet everywhere was the same: the streets all led back to the main road to the palace in concentric circles. His earlier worries of finding Shaharazad seemed foolish. It was impossible *not* to reach the palace.

Even more guards pursued him now. People pointed as he ran past. Sweat seeped into his eyes and his lungs ached. The noise of the market indicated he had chosen yet another wrong road. So much had gone badly. The fruit seller thought he was a thief, and Mohassin thought he was a traitor. Everywhere he was being chased by men with swords and he had lost his best chance of getting to Shari safely.

He made for an empty alley, a narrow track behind a cluster of living quarters. The alley appeared deserted, but there would be no escape routes out the side if he entered. Walls rose on all sides with only the odd door frame to break up the mud-brick barriers until the exit on the other end. Still, it promised to lead away from the palace, and Yeats took it.

He was only a few yards in when a palace guard entered from the opposite end.

Yeats froze. The dust from Yeats's feet swirled ahead with the breeze and rushed the guard's face like an insult. The soldier spat, wiping his lips. Then he raised his scimitar and charged.

This time, Yeats's feet failed him. The guard was too fast and Yeats was exhausted. As he teetered toward the wall, sweat trickled into his mouth. He raised his fists. It would take more than a single punch to knock this guard down. *Will my head roll*

like a cabbage spilled from a cart? Will I feel anything?
The beggar's laughter rolled insanely through his
thoughts.

The guard swung and Yeats ducked. Splinters
of wood stung the back of his neck. More footsteps
sounded in the alley. Yeats punched and missed.
Then someone delivered a terrible blow to the
side of his head and he fell down, quickly losing
consciousness.

Yeats moaned. His vision was blurry and his head
hurt.

"You all right?"

The question came from someone near his
feet. Yeats opened his eyes a little wider. Someone
peered at him from behind a set of bars. Light
streamed in from a grate in the ceiling.

Yeats tried to sit up. "Everything hurts," he
murmured. A wave of dizziness washed over him
and he lay down again in the dirty straw. "Where
am I?"

"Prison. Well, it's more of a hole, really. It's
not the palace. We're in the town." The speaker

was a boy, and Yeats squinted to see more of him and their surroundings. It was not quite a cell— more like a cave carved out of the rock. The straw beneath him was black with mold and made him sneeze.

Yeats slapped his knee. "I don't have time for this. Can't believe I risked the alley! I could be safely on my way. I wish I had the panther's help again."

"A panther!" The boy crouched and leaned toward him. When he dipped into the shaft of light, Yeats saw his shaved head and black skin.

"You're not from around here, are you?" Yeats ventured. He sat up slowly.

The boy glanced at the grille overhead, revealing a split bottom lip. "No, I'm not. How did you know?"

Yeats dabbed at the blood around his eye. "You're wearing running shoes," he said.

The boy gasped. "Yes! So you're from . . . where I come from? It's all gone foggy."

Yeats nodded. "You're caught in a spell," he explained. "You must have wished something in a book, and it went bad. It's happened before. I'm trying to rescue . . ."

A bearded face suddenly appeared at the grille above them. "Silence!" the guard growled. The boy ducked as if he feared something would be thrown at him. Then he stood, arched his back, and spat. A series of wild curses came from the other side of the grille.

Dirt and bits of straw fell through the grate and peppered Yeats's face before the guards' footsteps were heard retreating overhead.

"Good shot, Roland!"

Although the boy smiled, the glitter of tears on his cheeks indicated another sort of feeling. "How do you know my name?"

Yeats glanced at the grille and crawled to the bars. "We have to get out of here. You've been in the story longer than you should. Khan is searching for you."

"Khan," the boy repeated.

Yeats nodded. "He's not gentle, but he is on your side. I'm supposed to tell him I've seen you." He sighed. "Not much chance of that now. Not unless he figures out where we are. And he hasn't had much luck so far. He has to spend most of his time in the garden."

Roland licked at his split lip. "When I got here, there was a snake charmer at the marketplace. Amazing! He made the snake rise out of the basket and people threw coins at him. One of the coins rolled toward me and I picked it up. Before I could give it back the snake charmer went crazy. He claimed I was a thief and the next thing I knew I was thrown in here."

Yeats leaned against the bars. "How long?"

"I'm not sure. I can see the stars at night and I've tried to keep count. Nothing to read and nothing to do so I sleep all the time. It's cold and I've only had bread and water. It makes you tired." He nodded at the grille. "They keep saying they're going to hang me."

The boys were silent for a few moments, pondering their misfortune. Eventually Yeats said, "Well, you're not a thief. You're not even from this story. You and I belong in another world. I've got to bring back a girl; that's why I'm here. She's lost the same as you, only she thinks she's the vizier's daughter. She's very smart, but I can't seem to convince her."

"A girl, is it?" Roland asked curiously.

"It's not like that," Yeats replied.

"You sure? You sounded kind of wistful."

The boys locked eyes and Yeats knew instantly he could trust him.

"I like her," Yeats finally said. "We've only just met, but she's so different."

"Pretty?"

"Yep."

Roland pursed his lips. "Think she likes you?"

"Not sure. Maybe," said Yeats. "Never can tell with girls."

"Well," Roland continued, "you might want to find out, 'cause if she does, that might convince her to go with you."

"Good point," Yeats said. "Thanks."

Roland offered his hand through the bars. "I'm glad you're here. You're the only good thing that's happened in a long time." They shook hands and did not let go, white and black fingers clasped tightly.

"What's your name?"

"Yeats. Where are you from?"

Roland closed his eyes. He scratched at the tiny tufts of his shaved head. "France," he said slowly.

"I've seen it from across the Channel when we took a vacation to England," said Yeats. "You don't sound French."

"We just moved. My dad got a job. I've got a big room with lots of books." Roland smiled. "My aunt sent me a box—a trunk—full of books." He gingerly touched his lip. "The panther was in the trunk too! I thought he was just a normal bookend. There was also a really old book. I wanted to read it right away, but it was late. And my mom said I had to wait. When my parents went to sleep I opened up the box again and there was Khan, twirling his tail around and around." Roland gathered another gob of spit and hit the far wall.

"You're good at that," Yeats said.

"Practice."

They were quiet for a few minutes. Yeats's thoughts drifted to France, then home. "We've got to get out!" Yeats groaned. "Shari will be waiting for me at midnight. And my family's life depends on it." He winced the moment the words were out, remembering Roland's promised punishment. "Sorry. I forgot. Don't worry, though. We'll think of something, right?"

At that moment, the grille opened. A guard descended the ladder carrying a small water skin. Yeats and Roland stood and took a step away from the bars.

The man spat at Roland. Roland spat back, aiming at the man's head. The guard ducked and laughed. Then he turned and smiled wickedly at Yeats. "It's the gallows, boy!" he leered. "The gallows!"

Gallows!

"We're going to hang you, traitor. Midnight, tonight!"

Yeats's knees buckled.

"The other one dies tomorrow. And about time too. He's eaten enough bread for a thief."

The guard tossed the water skin into the cell where it slapped and skidded along the stone floor. "Enjoy your last meal!" he laughed. Instead of climbing the ladder, the guard exited through a door in the wall beside the cells. When it slammed shut, Yeats fell forward on his hands and knees. Tears splashed onto the stones. His stomach lurched and he threw up. When he regained his senses, Roland was whispering.

"Hey, Yeats! Easy now. Come here."

Yeats managed to crawl to the bars. His shoulders shook and he wiped his mouth.

Roland patted his back. "Courage, Yeats. Get the skin there and have a drink."

Although he barely heard the words, he followed his instructions.

"The guard's been saying that to me for three days," Roland said. "And I've still got my neck!"

"Thanks." Yeats sniffed. "But I don't think he was bluffing. I've done more than steal a coin."

"Can't be too bad. I've nailed that guard ten times. He gets excited when I miss. He's a lousy shot."

After another sip, Yeats sighed. "Yeah, but I'm trying to kidnap the vizier's daughter."

Roland slid down the bars and the boys sat,

back-to-back, treasuring the comfort while it lasted.

"If we were in the same cell," Roland said a few minutes later, "we might pretend we were sleeping. When the guard comes—it's always the same one, and he hates me—we could knock him over or something."

"And then what?" Yeats grumbled.

"Well, we could take his sword!"

"And how would that help? Have you ever attacked someone with a sword? These are warriors! They know their business. I've never even held a sword."

Roland slapped the ground. "Still, one of us might get out!"

A guard walked across the grille and they both stiffened. His shadow washed over them and disappeared.

"What happens if we die here?" Yeats murmured. A thought flickered in his mind and he sat up. "Can we die? Roland! Maybe we can't die! It's a story, so how can we die in this story if we belong in a different world?"

Roland took a sip of water and then said, "Not sure why you're so worried about what will happen in two different places. This one's bad enough. And look at your leg. You better tighten the rag. Blood's leaking through."

Yeats stared at his leg for a long moment. "The pain is real enough. If I can feel this kind of pain, then . . ." He looked wildly up at Roland. "Then death will probably be real too!"

Roland started to speak, then stopped. Yeats buried his face in his hands.

14

THE
POOL

Shaharazad knelt and dipped her fingers in the cool water. There was no one else around and so she had the pool to herself. It was one of her favorite places in the palace. She could see the servants bustling in and out of the kitchens, and if she squinted, she could even glimpse a door that opened to the outside, to the market and the wide world beyond.

Each day she hoped she might see something that would reveal what was going on in the city. But she was not allowed to step past the raging bulls on the floor. The guards knew it, too, and kept a close eye on her when she came near. Whenever weepers went by the entrance a guard always went out and moved them away and out of hearing.

However, this day her mind was full and she rarely looked toward the servants' door. The air was cooler near the pool, and it was the best place to read without interruption in the late afternoon. The pool was also a favorite location for Rawiya, who never missed an opportunity to gossip with friends in the kitchens. Shaharazad and Rawiya had fallen into the comfortable habit of coming to the pool most afternoons. Rawiya visited and Shaharazad read.

On this occasion, however, she had a hard time relaxing. No sooner had she begun to read when she found her mind wandering.

"Yeats," she murmured. She thought of him standing in the shadows beneath the tree only the night before. "How you stir my memory," she said. It was the strangest feeling. There were pictures in her mind that were clearer than detailed paintings, of places and people she did not know. They rose up like ghosts every time she thought of Yeats. Since their first meeting she had felt a growing sense of anticipation that something terribly significant was about to happen. She began to believe that his coming to the garden and her finding him was no accident but rather providential.

"And what news will you bring tonight?" she whispered. "What will you tell me? Have you kept your word? Will you tell me why the people weep?"

She laid the book aside and leaned over the water. When her eyes locked with those of her reflection she gasped, for at that very moment she felt a tug, as if her whole body was being pulled forward. She reached out to steady herself against a statue. At the same time she heard a voice, a boy's voice, echoing across the pool. "I wish! I wish!" it said. The voice rolled over her like a wind. And then it was gone.

She sat up and looked around her, but all was as it had been before the voice had spoken. She took several deep breaths and then leaned over the water again, this time a little more cautiously. She did not let go of the statue's base.

"'Mysteries and wonders too great to compare!'" she quoted from a favorite poet. Then she passed a hand over her eyes. What had just happened? A vision? A ghost?

"My lady?"

Scrambling to keep her balance, Shaharazad pulled herself back. "Rawiya!" she said. "You startled me."

"What were you doing?" asked the older woman.

"I was . . . I heard . . ." Her heart was troubled. It suddenly occurred to her that whenever she thought of Yeats strange memories arose. And then the ghostlike voice appeared. She shivered. What if Yeats was not safe? What if he was not good but evil? The thought was disturbing. "I was looking at my reflection," she said slowly. "I wanted . . ."

"My lady," Rawiya interrupted. "Something is amiss. I was not allowed in the kitchen and was told to take you back to your room. Immediately."

Shaharazad's head shot up. For a moment she wanted to run into the kitchen and find out what was happening. Then her mind settled. Whether or not Yeats kept his end of their agreement, she at least would keep hers. She felt her confidence returning. Of course Yeats was good. She knew it in her heart. And he was coming at midnight to answer her questions. She would be ready. Aloud, all she said was, "Of course."

On their way back to her chamber they met a pair of guards running in the direction of the pool. Shaharazad had never seen guards running in the palace before. Back in her chamber, Rawiya closed the door behind them and locked it.

15

A TALE WORTH REMEMBERING

William held the book in his lap. A tear splashed onto the pages.

"William?" Faith said. "What in heaven's name just happened? Where did Mr. Sutcliff go? You'd better have an explanation."

Her husband did not turn from the pages. He merely whispered, "Why can't I go? Why can't I help my son?"

"Go where, William?" The blood drained from her face. Where was Yeats?

Gran touched the spot where, only moments before, two long-forgotten bookends stood watch over her library. "Don't be afraid, Faith. Instead, be patient."

"Mum!" Faith stammered. "Did you not just see? Mr. Sutcliff was standing here, right there, and reading *that* book. He disappeared! And what on earth was he doing yelling at a bookend?"

Gran clasped her hands to her face. "Yes! Yes! It was wonderful. I've always known Mr. Sutcliff would figure it out."

"Wonderful?" Faith gaped, flabbergasted. "William?"

He ran his fingers over the pages. "I can't get in."

"Get in where?! Are you both mad?"

Gran rested her hand on Faith's shoulder. "Faith. Don't turn away—look at me, girl! I know you are afraid. You have a right to be. But rest assured that while there may be forces out of our control, we just gained one for our side. Mr. Sutcliff is there now, I'm sure of it. He'll find Yeats. And your husband is not mad. Neither am I."

Faith was speechless.

"Listen to me," Gran continued. "You will need to see this with your heart and not just your eyes. You're a smart girl. Always have been. I'm proud of you. But all your intelligence can't help you if you won't see what is happening. Three people have disappeared, one of them before your very eyes. You are witnessing a marvel. If you can't believe it for William, and Lord knows he needs you to, then at least do it for your son. Can you?"

Faith felt ill.

"Can you?" Gran repeated.

Faith clutched her stomach. It was late afternoon. She could not imagine making it through the night without knowing something about Yeats.

Gran waited patiently.

Slowly she turned to her mother-in-law. Without looking at her husband she said, "I'll do anything to get my son back."

16

THE GALLOWS

Yeats awoke to darkness and cold bars pressed against his back.

"Roland?"

"Hmmm?"

"Roland! What time is it?"

"Don't know, exactly. I think it's still daytime, if that's what you are wondering."

"It is?"

"Yep. But they put a carpet over the grate. They've never done that before."

Yeats kicked the bars. "They're trying to frighten us. Not letting us know when it's midnight. Maggots!" he yelled. "Khan! Khan! Roland's here! Come and save us!"

The carpet lifted and the guard's face appeared. He traced his finger across his throat. The carpet fell back into place and they were plunged into darkness once again.

Yeats fell back with a grunt. It was no good. Khan was prevented from roaming in the daytime. He knew with growing certainty that he would die, at twelve years old, inside a book! He kicked at the bars again. They would not take him easily. His family, Shari, Roland, all needed him alive. No, he would make his captors pay before they got him.

"We've got to think of something!" Yeats said.

"I'm not so sure that yelling—" Roland was interrupted by the sound of a key scraping in a lock. Both boys peered into the darkness.

The door, from which the guard had exited earlier, creaked open, as someone took great pains to keep the hinges quiet. Yeats glanced at the carpeted grille above but no light appeared.

The boys clasped hands through the bars.

"Can't see a thing," Roland whispered. "We're going to have to fight."

"There could be more than one," Yeats said.

Footsteps sounded on the stone floor: cautious footfalls.

"Maybe the guard was bluffing," Roland squeaked. "Maybe they're coming for us!"

Yeats understood the plan all too clearly now. The carpet blocked out the light for the benefit of the guards. They were going to hang the boys in broad daylight.

Roland gritted his teeth. "I won't let go! They'll have to rip us apart! I'll kick 'em; I'll bite 'em!" Roland was working himself into a frenzy.

Yeats drew from his friend's strength and raised a fist. "Aim a punch for the nose and kick between the legs."

A key rattled in the door of Yeats's cell. They heard a man shifting his feet in the straw. Yeats prepared to lunge. The man entered but left the door open. There came a scratching sound and a match burst into life. The crackle of light revealed a wrinkled, anxious face framed by a turban with a long strand of white hair coiling down one side.

"Mr. Sutcliff!" Yeats exclaimed.

The old man gripped his shoulder. "Found you!" he said.

"How did you . . . ?" Yeats began.

"No time for that, my boy. Have you seen her? Have you seen Shaharazad?"

Yeats nodded as the match blew out.

"Good boy." Mr. Sutcliff lit another. "You'd best come now. And do hurry!"

Yeats wiped his sweaty forehead. He looked hopefully beyond the cell.

"No," Mr. Sutcliff answered. "Your parents are not here."

Tears filled Yeats's eyes. "They must be so scared."

"They are," agreed Mr. Sutcliff. "But not the way you think. Apparently story time works differently from our own. You'd scarcely been gone an hour when I arrived in the story. How long have you been here?"

"I got here yesterday," answered Yeats. "So much has happened. Mr. Sutcliff! Mom needs to see this. Everything Dad said was true. He's not crazy."

The old man grunted. "No, indeed. *You* are the key, my boy. If ever your family is to be whole again, we need you to do the greatest part."

There was a scraping sound from above and light poured into the cell.

"Come, my boy! We've tarried long enough."

"Wait!" Yeats cried. "My friend Roland—we must rescue him too."

The guard yelled and several more faces appeared.

"There's no time, Yeats!" Mr. Sutcliff wrenched him from the cell with surprising strength.

"I'll get you out, Roland," he gasped. "I promise."

"Yeats! Don't forget me." Roland stretched out his hand.

"I won't! I'll tell Khan. Roland! If you get out . . . find Rosemary Townend in Maine, USA. That's my gran. Remember it!"

"Rosemary Townend, Maine, USA," Roland repeated. "I got it."

Yeats slipped on the straw-covered stone as he was propelled out of the cell by Mr. Sutcliff. There was light ahead and the matches were no longer needed. They raced past the guard climbing down the ladder, his sandaled foot inches from their heads, toward the door in the wall. The door slammed behind with a grinding shudder, and Mr. Sutcliff hurried them down the torch-lit corridor. All at once, two shadows detached from the walls and blocked the way.

"Look out!" Yeats cried.

"Quiet," hushed one of the shadows. The figure leaned into the light.

Yeats caught his breath.

"Skin, at yer service." The pirate nodded, as did his partner.

Disbelieving, Yeats looked from one to the other.

"Carry on, Sutcliff!" Bones growled. "We can expect more trouble if we dally."

The passage opened into an overgrown garden. Yeats blinked in the brightness while his eyes adjusted. A grisly sight appeared: a long rope hung from a tree at the center of the garden, the afternoon sun casting the shadow of a noose over the broken ground.

Yeats came to a halt. "We've got to go back," he puffed. "For Roland." He made to turn, but Skin pushed him forward.

"No, you don't. We've a wish to fulfill and ye won't be stopping us so easily as that."

"A wish?" Yeats asked breathlessly. "But I . . ."

"Not yer wish, landlubber!" The pirate glared at Mr. Sutcliff. "His."

"I don't understand," said Yeats. "Why can't we rescue Roland?"

"We'll do what we can, son," Mr. Sutcliff said soberly. "That's my promise. And I do not give promises lightly. But if we're caught here, none of us will make it out alive. Think of what that would mean for your family."

Yeats could have punched one of the pirates in frustration, but Mr. Sutcliff's words were true enough and so he hurried along. They followed a path that skirted the garden, and Yeats looked back frequently. It crossed his mind that he should break away and go back for Roland. But the pirates seemed to anticipate his movements. Skin remained in position at the rear, the sound of his wooden leg thumping the ground as a reminder.

Bones navigated the alleys, avoiding the main roads. They passed a garden enclosed by a low whitewashed wall and filled with statues. The pirates stopped frequently to listen for sounds of pursuit.

"Stay close," Bones whispered. "Best lay low till they've finished searching for us."

They reached a row of homes in disrepair. The mud-brick walls had been shattered in places and broken tiles clinked wherever they walked. Yeats kept a lookout for the dark-robed palace guards, and the pirates flinched at every sound, their weapons at the ready. They stopped at the back of a ruined home, and Mr. Sutcliff patted Yeats on the back.

"Don't worry, my boy. These two know their business."

Skin pushed open a wooden door with a gaping hole at its center. "After you, yer highness," he said drily to Yeats. Pieces of the roof and walls lay everywhere and the collapsing upper floor revealed the open sky.

"Is it safe?" Yeats hardly dared to breathe lest he cause a house avalanche.

"Hope not," Skin answered gruffly. "Keep 'em all away."

Mr. Sutcliff pulled out a water skin. "Here, Yeats." Yeats gulped down the water gratefully and then took a longer look at his rescuer. In the dilapidated ruins Mr. Sutcliff looked much different than in the upper room at Gran's house. Gone was the stiff figure he'd brought tea. Now he moved fluidly, purposefully, and with a great deal more authority. He seemed to understand Yeats's stare.

"I've waited twenty years for this, my boy," he said and adjusted his turban. "I've always wanted my story to end with an adventure." His smile faded. "And truly—happily ever after."

"I think I know what you wished for," Yeats said.

Mr. Sutcliff raised his eyebrows.

"You wished for the pirates to help you bring back your granddaughter."

He smirked. "Good guess and very nearly true." He leaned closer and whispered, "I wished for their undivided aid in rescuing both of you! I'm a firm believer in two for ones. It's another reason why I could not wait for your young friend Roland. The pirates are not bound to him."

"I wish I'd been a little smarter," admitted Yeats. "I would have wished for something more specific and saved us all this trouble."

The old man cocked an eye knowingly. "They are not particularly helpful or friendly, are they, our pirates? But don't you worry. I'll keep them to task." He sighed and stared at the unhappy sight around them. "We are standing in what was likely a wealthy merchant's home. The remains of a family portrait are lying on the floor, there. I'd guess this merchant fell out of favor with royalty. It was common practice to turn a home into rubble if you displeased the King."

Skin said, "Can't say I'd want to fall afoul of 'im."

"Precisely!" Mr. Sutcliff agreed.

"What about the people who lived here?" Yeats whispered.

Mr. Sutcliff adjusted his turban before responding. "I'd wager they came to an exotic end. Best not ponder such things when we have our own dangers ahead. And we have work to do. But first, some news! Tell me about Shaharazad."

Skin took up position at the opposite end of the house, where the remains of another door led into sunlight. His sword reflected the light, and his swashbuckling sea cape and hat filled Yeats with courage.

"I've seen her! I've spoken to her!"

"Is she in danger?" Mr. Sutcliff asked.

"I don't know. She wants to know why the townspeople are weeping. She does not know that the maidens are dying. She hired me to find out." He frowned thoughtfully and then added, "We agreed to meet tonight. At midnight, at her chamber in the palace."

Mr. Sutcliff paced, crunching bits of tile underfoot. "This works in our favor. But how do we get to her? You seem to be a wanted man."

Wincing, Yeats added, "The palace guards know that I'm trying to meet her. And they know when too. I'm afraid I ruined everything."

Mr. Sutcliff rubbed his chin. "Unfortunate. I hoped our prison break would be less conspicuous. You're a boy, after all, not a political prisoner. But apparently you've become a celebrity."

"Mohassin, the royal cook, told them everything," Yeats admitted. "He thinks I'm a traitor—that I intend to hurt Shaharazad."

For a long moment Mr. Sutcliff studied Yeats. Then he said, "It is imperative that we reach her. She must be convinced to come home. The pirates are firm about that. They will not bring her back unless she chooses to break her own spell." His eyebrows knit in deep concern. "And we engage in a difficult task. My granddaughter chose this story purposefully, for it parallels her own: a girl of her own ancestry, called upon to face tragedy, solve a great problem, and create a happy ending for all."

Yeats could only stare at the ground. He knew how difficult it was. He had already spoken with her once.

Mr. Sutcliff hurried on. "She must be brought to her senses quickly for I cannot ask you to risk yourself much longer. We are in a dangerous story, my boy, with many pitfalls." Then, in a different tone he said, "Yet, there is one thing I know for certain: we cannot claim to have lived life unless we have taken risks. And I've great faith in you, my boy. Shari will listen to you."

Yeats thought about that. His father had not taken any great risks for years until their return to Gran's house. And look what had happened!

Mr. Sutcliff pursed his lips. "The trick is to find the spark of memory that makes her long for home. We've got to break that wish!"

Skin gave a snort from his guard post.

"We mustn't lose heart," the old man said. "She trusts you, or she would never agree to meet you. Therein lies our hope. We must at all costs keep your meeting."

"But we have to rescue Roland as well!" Yeats exclaimed.

"I've been thinking about him," said Mr. Sutcliff. "There was little time to tell you while we escaped the cells. That boy will do as the story says. We can't be rescuing characters."

"But he's not a character!" Yeats protested. "He doesn't belong here. He's from our world."

Mr. Sutcliff stared sternly. "Did he tell you that?"

Yeats nodded. "I promised. I can't leave him."

The older man pursed his lips thoughtfully. "You're right, of course. It's a fine quality to think of a friend in need. I should know. And you're quite certain he's not a character?" asked Mr. Sutcliff.

"Yes."

"Curious." He pointed to the pirates. "Do you know about this?"

"No." Skin shook his head. "But t'ain't like we are the only magicals." His partner glared at him and stopped him from saying anything more.

"We'll do what we can, Yeats. That's the best I can offer," Mr. Sutcliff said. "But in my limited experience, I would suggest there may be someone after him other than us. He may not be as alone as you think."

Yeats agreed. It was the best he could ask for under the circumstances. And there was a chance he could tell Khan if they made it to Shaharazad.

Mr. Sutcliff resumed pacing. "And now for my granddaughter. We will need different costumes. We might find something at the market. Have you any money?"

Yeats held up his coins still folded into the waistline of his underwear.

"Excellent." Mr. Sutcliff rubbed his hands together, then turned to Bones. "Has anyone ever told you that you would look dashing in black?"

17

A ROGUE
AND A VILLAIN

Poetry, a little food, and reading filled the remainder of Shaharazad's day in the confines of her room. Her father did not come and she made a great deal of fuss, disguising her true anxiety. The palace was astir and it was maddening not to know what was going on both inside and outside of the walls. Rawiya clucked over her more than usual, so much so that Shaharazad decided if she heard "posture, my lady" one more time she would be forced to give her maid a good shaking. What she needed was some time to practice with her sword, but with Rawiya around there was no chance for it.

By sunset Shaharazad could scarcely contain

her impatience. She had had enough of pretending and wanted to wait out the time alone. She begged Rawiya for a dose of cordial from the kitchen to ease her headache, and mercifully her maid left. Shaharazad leapt to her windowsill and peered into the darkening gloom of the town.

"Hurry, Yeats," she whispered. "I am anxious for your news." She smiled briefly. "And your familiar face."

Rawiya returned with a small flask of cordial and fairly cast it on the table. Her face was pale and her hands shook when she poured the drink.

"Are you ill, Rawiya?"

"No, my lady."

"You are shaking."

Rawiya gasped, then whispered frantically, "Guards are doubled at every entrance and two wait outside your door. An assistant cook told me that a villain tried to enter the palace!" She was as near to clucking as a startled chicken. "And he was trying to get to your chamber!"

Shaharazad sat straight up. "Was he caught?"

"No! Three tried to apprehend him, including a

palace guard, but he overpowered them! The cook's nose! It was broken. It must be a fierce rogue." Rawiya shook her finger. "We must be cautious!"

The girl nodded thoughtfully. "Did the cook describe this villain?"

Her maidservant frowned. "That is the strangest of things. The cook claimed the rogue was a beast who could hurl stones the size of his head with the accuracy of an archer. But the royal food taster swore he was no more than a boy! A cabbage seller confessed the same. And Mustafa the beggar won't utter a word, which is something to be said in itself."

Shaharazad smothered a smile. So! Mohassin must have bribed the beggar to silence. Yeats had made it to the kitchen! She frowned. But what of the palace guard? *Oh, please be safe!*

Composing herself, Shaharazad took her maid's hands. "Rawiya. If there is a rogue loose in the palace—and a dangerous one at that—then I want you back in your home with your husband. I will be safe with guards outside my door. Besides, it is late. And you have already stayed too long."

Tears formed in the woman's eyes. "Sweet Shaharazad. You never think of yourself."

"I insist," the girl said.

Rawiya did not move.

"I command," Shaharazad said firmly.

Rawiya stood slowly. "Thank you, my lady. I will be here at dawn for your bath."

"As always, Rawiya."

When the maid reached the door, Shaharazad called out, "Rawiya. Do I . . . I mean . . . is my hair pretty tonight?"

Rawiya looked up in surprise.

18

MIDNIGHT

For old bookends, Skin and Bones still had a knack for stealth. Keeping to shadows, they maneuvered through the darkened streets. In black robes and turbans the pirates made convincing palace guards. Even Skin's peg leg was perfectly hidden beneath the swirling garments.

"As long as they don't speak, it might work," Mr. Sutcliff said quietly to Yeats.

The wailing had started again and covered the sound of their passing. "Steady on," Mr. Sutcliff whispered as weeping erupted from one house and made them all jump. "What a mournful sound. No wonder my granddaughter worries for the city."

"Quiet!" Bones hissed. They all pressed against

the wall. The dusty alleys crisscrossed with cobbled roads as they made their way up to the palace. Bones leapt onto a wall and stood in the moonlight, his robes billowing in the gusty desert wind.

"We're too far to port. Bear starboard-side. Wind's picking up!" he whispered.

Yeats chewed the inside of his cheek. Since leaving the ruined house he could not shake the feeling that they were being followed. Yet every time he turned, the streets were deserted.

He thought of Shaharazad. So much had happened to him that there hadn't been much time to wonder about her since the morning. She was so determined. Her eyes commanded without words. But would she listen? Would she believe him? Mr. Sutcliff had such faith in him. There had to be a way of convincing her. Yeats wrapped his tunic tighter and stepped into the street behind Bones.

Closer to the palace the roads were paved with smooth luminescent stones that gleamed in the moonlight. It gave the streets an eerie glow that made Yeats peer anxiously into the shadows. The rasp of Mr. Sutcliff's labored breathing sounded far too loud. The brooding watchfulness of the vacant streets made Yeats's skin crawl.

A moment later two watchmen carrying lanterns stepped into the street from an alley. The pirates pressed against a wall. Yeats held his breath and focused on the figures, only a stone's throw from their meager hiding place. Ahead, with the promise of further danger, the palace loomed.

It was a cat that gave them away. Mr. Sutcliff inadvertently stepped on its tail. The cat yowled and shot across the road, directly alerting the watchmen.

"Dead man's hand!" exclaimed Skin.

"Ho there! What's your business?" cried a watchman.

"What should we do?" Yeats whispered.

Mr. Sutcliff gripped Yeats's arm and pushed him toward Bones. "Hold the boy out in front. Tell them you've caught the traitor!"

Bones grasped Yeats roughly. "Er, we caught the scurvy dog . . ."

"Traitor!" Mr. Sutcliff hissed.

"Er . . . traitor," Bones finished.

The watchmen stepped into the middle of the street. "Who are you?""

"Palace guard, ya poltroon!"

The watchmen drew their scimitars.

Skin's face caught the moonlight. He grinned and pushed Yeats away. "Go on, lad. Git! We'll take it from here. Ye too," he added to Mr. Sutcliff. "We'll catch up."

Mr. Sutcliff seized Yeats's arm and hurried up the street. "Come on."

"What about them?" Yeats craned his neck to see the watchmen advance menacingly toward the pirates, fanning out with scimitars pointing.

"They're pirates. I've no doubt we'll see them again. I dare say they're enjoying themselves," said Mr. Sutcliff.

Another patrol marched past the entrance of an empty road and Mr. Sutcliff waited until their footsteps died away. Yeats searched the shadows.

"We're being followed," he finally whispered.

Mr. Sutcliff swung around. "Did you hear something?"

"Not sure. I sense it."

"You may just be hearing the echoes of our pirates and the watch. They were having quite a fight!"

Yeats shook his head. "I don't think so."

Mr. Sutcliff poked his head around the wall. "Can you find your way to her, Yeats?"

"I'm not sure, sir. I know we ran across a garden lawn . . ."

"So you were in the palace garden."

"Yes."

"I think I can get you there."

Yeats frowned. "You know this place, sir?"

Footsteps made them fall silent. They waited for stillness before moving on. The wailing from the town had ceased.

"It's late," Mr. Sutcliff whispered. "Families are finally asleep. What a dreadful existence! They have such courage to keep going despite all the tragedy that has befallen them. This way, my boy."

Yeats pulled back. "How do you know where to go?"

The old man sniffed. "I've read Collfield's unexpurgated translation a hundred times since

Shari disappeared. I've also read every version of the *Arabian Nights* in your grandmother's library. My memory holds detailed maps of this palace. And so it should! I've been trying to get here for twenty years. The gardens are this way."

He led them farther into the palace grounds, past fountains, statues, and tall pillars. Small oil lamps placed at regular intervals along the walkways illuminated the route. Mr. Sutcliff froze.

"There!" he whispered. An enormous gateway loomed before them. Against the marble floor waves of shimmering light reflected their faces. "Doors of pure gold!"

Yeats's skin prickled. Two guards stood at attention on either side of the mighty portal, their bare scimitars balanced on their shoulders.

"This could be a problem." Mr. Sutcliff tapped his lips as if he held his pipe.

"Now what?" asked Yeats. "They'll kill us if we walk up to them!"

"Yes, indeed!" Mr. Sutcliff agreed.

"Do you have a plan, sir?"

"A plan?" Mr. Sutcliff raised an eyebrow. "Well,

we are *in a story*. Something will present itself. Have you forgotten? We will have action. There is no story unless things happen."

Yeats whispered desperately, "Are we just going to—" The cold tip of steel pressed against his neck. From the corners of his eyes he glimpsed black robes swishing around his feet. Whiskers tickled his ear.

"Ye two are so loud I could have run ye through with eye patches over both me eyes!" Skin grinned.

"There, you see?" Mr. Sutcliff smiled knowingly. "Something had to happen. Thankfully it was in our favor. You two do look like palace guards. And your timing is perfect. We are going to need you to get beyond those rather intimidating figures at the gate."

Bones grimaced. "Don't push yer luck, Sutcliff."

"Ah, but we must!" said the older man. "Now listen!"

A few moments later, Yeats and his companions walked brazenly into the light of the palace gateway. The sensation was almost as horrifying as waiting to be hanged in a dark cell. Yeats took comfort from Skin and Bones, although they held him so tightly his arms ached. At the same time, the sight of the real guards, whose scimitars dwarfed the pirates' cutlasses, made his knees tremble.

"We have the traitor!" Bones declared before either guard spoke. "And here is the merchant who delivered him into our hands." Mr. Sutcliff bowed.

"We are taking them to the King!" Bones added.

The guards glanced at each other. "Password!"

There was a second of silence and then Yeats was on the ground, having been dropped simultaneously by both pirates. He looked up in time to see Skin head-butt his opponent over a hedge. Bones wrestled the other guard. Skin leapt to his partner's aid and gripped the guard by the neck, smacking him on the top of his head with the hilt of his cutlass.

Skin and Bones stood panting above the motionless man. Yeats looked around to see if any further alarm had been raised.

"Marvelous!" Mr. Sutcliff congratulated. "Quickly, now. We haven't much time. It's almost midnight!"

With a creak and a shudder, the doors opened

at the pirates' shove, revealing the sculptured plants and the open lawn where Yeats had first found Shaharazad. Mr. Sutcliff pressed against the hedge.

"Guards everywhere! Your cook has spread the word."

Yeats nodded. "How will we get to her?"

Mr. Sutcliff grunted. "If I know that girl she will make a way for you. As for our part, we must get you as close to her chamber as possible. After that, it is up to you."

Yeats's heart thumped. He pointed and grimaced. "That's the entrance to her room—where the guards are standing. They weren't there last night."

"Not sure if we can take four of 'em quietly," Bones whispered soberly.

Mr. Sutcliff was thinking, his eyes sternly focused on the guards who separated him from his granddaughter.

"Have any ideas, sir?" Yeats asked.

Mr. Sutcliff turned to Yeats. He took his hands in his own wrinkly palms. "You're a good boy, Yeats," he said. "You've done your father proud. Always remember that you are a visitor here, sharing an adventure. But you belong somewhere else. Never forget it. Can you do that? Get her home, boy! And may your young friend Roland find his way to safety as well."

Yeats nodded uncertainly.

Then without another word the old man released Yeats and stepped into the moonlit garden.

"Scurvy dog!" Bones hissed after him. "Are ye daft, man?"

Mr. Sutcliff paid no heed. Instead he made for the center of the grounds where Shaharazad's fountain splashed and foamed. The guards saw him at once and shouted.

"A ruse!" Skin whispered. "Very brave and very stupid! Go on, lad. He's cleared the way. Run for it!"

Yeats held his ground. "But what about Mr. Sutcliff?"

Bones shifted his cutlass. "He's not alone. Come on, Skin!" The pirates broke from their cover.

The path to Shaharazad was open and Yeats sprang forward.

Green eyes gleamed, unnoticed, from the hedge.

19

THE
DIVERSION

Shaharazad pressed her ear to the door. After a long minute a guard coughed. She turned and paced to the window. She had doused the lamps long ago and it was moonlight that lit her her face as she raised it to the stars. "A night for poets," she murmured.

Her gaze fell from the sky to the darkness of the carpeted floor. Something stirred her soul but she could not place it. Many an hour she had spent planning and plotting a way out of her confines. And then Yeats had appeared in the garden, under the nose of Khan and the guards, wanting to rescue her. Why he wanted to rescue her—and from what—she could not imagine, but

it was a noble desire, was it not? With his help she felt certain that she could discover the pain of the people, the cause of their weeping, and then set about saving them.

"'Adventure finds the thirsty heart,'" she quoted softly. "And how my heart thirsts!" She rose from the window and went to her bed. Lifting the cushions, she felt for the sword. The hilt settled comfortably in her hand as she cut the darkness with practiced skill. Rawiya was not in the chamber after dark and so missed Shaharazad's military drills and swordsmanship exercises each night.

Shaharazad returned the weapon to the cushions. She found her tinderbox and placed it at the door. Rummaging through her clothes, she found a scarf of considerable length. "As good a fuse as any," she murmured. With a last deep breath, she reached for the tinderbox.

20

WILLIAM'S SON

In the garden, Yeats once again found himself pinned to the earth by Khan. The panther growled.

His breath strained, Yeats whispered, "I've seen Roland. He's in the town. In prison. There is a garden and gallows right next to it."

The green eyes winked shut. The giant paws pushed heavily on Yeats's chest.

"It's true! I can prove it. Roland found you in a trunk," he stammered at last. "He got it from his aunt. He has running shoes, and now he . . . he's my friend."

Khan's breath blasted in Yeats's face. "What happened?"

Wincing, Yeats looked across the lawn. "He was caught for stealing. I was caught too. The guards said they would hang him in the morning. They wanted to kill me tonight but the pirates—"

"How many guards?" Khan stepped off him and began to pace.

"We only saw one. But there will be far more now that I've escaped."

Turning into the night, the giant cat coiled his muscles, ready to spring away.

"Khan!"

The panther faced him.

"Khan. Tell him I told you."

The panther's long tail flickered. "Be good to my mistress," he growled. "She has been good to me. And watch your back with those pirates!" The green eyes winked and the cat was gone.

There was no sign of the others when Yeats skidded across the lawn. The pirates and Mr. Sutcliff must have successfully drawn the guards deeper into the gardens. He made it to Shari's archway safely, his chest heaving. He peered down the corridor. A second later he flung himself back and pressed against the stones. Two guards approached with their swords drawn and looked anxiously up and down the corridor. From the garden came shouts and the clang of steel on steel.

Impossible! How could a kid take on two guards?

What should I do? he wondered. He couldn't risk running out into the open to look for the pirates or Mr. Sutcliff. And from the sounds of all the fighting, his friends were too busy to help him. Must be only minutes till midnight! Oh, where are those pirates?

He had just started concocting a plan involving throwing rocks at the guards when there was a burst of shouting. Yeats pressed his cheek against the cold stone and peeked around the corner. Flames appeared at the other end of the corridor. The guards whispered but did not leave their post. One of them pounded on Shaharazad's door.

"My lady! Please open. We must take you to another room. There is fire in the corridor." The door did not open. Smoke billowed and thickened and began to blow down the corridor. Yeats wrinkled his nose at the acrid smell. A few seconds later he covered his nose and mouth with his arm to breathe. The guards coughed and choked and still they pounded on her door. At last they ran out past Yeats with their eyes streaming. Smoke billowed out the archways and swirled around the pillars lining the corridor.

"Now or never!" Yeats muttered. With one arm flung over his mouth and nose he ran toward the fire. The smoke was too thick to see anything. Instead, he desperately felt along the wall. Almost out of air, he finally found the door. He was about to start pounding when something teased his memory. *One knock*, she had said. He rapped once with all his might. With no reserves left he opened his mouth to the awaiting smoke.

The door flung open and Yeats fell in. It closed behind him and a key turned in the lock. Yeats coughed and spluttered on the floor. His eyes streamed with tears that blurred his vision. He couldn't seem to get his breath.

A hand pressed a wet cloth against his face. "It will help," someone said, and he recognized

Shari's voice immediately. A moment later she propped up his head with a pillow. "Hurry, Yeats, and clear your eyes. I did not set much of a fire and the guards will return. They will break down the door to make certain I am well. There is, after all, a rogue loose in the palace!"

Yeats mopped his face and sucked in the clean air. When he opened his eyes, his mouth fell open at the extravagance of the room. Persian carpets covered the floor in a mosaic of rich purples and reds. Woven hangings, veils, and scarves of many colors latticed the walls. A couch littered with pillows stood near his head. At the opposite end of the room was a bed, majestically enfolded in veils and sheets. Several candles burned throughout the chamber, releasing the smell of cinnamon and other spices.

Shari was dressed in a nightgown and her unbraided hair fell past her shoulders. In her hands she held out a cup. "Drink," she said.

Yeats sipped the cool water. He was suddenly aware of his own dirty, smoke-covered tunic. "You look like Jasmine from *Aladdin*," he said.

She smiled. "That is an old tale."

Time slowed in the peace and luxury of her room. The water soothed his burning throat and her voice calmed his mind.

"My family loves stories and poetry," he said, suddenly feeling tired and longing for home. The carpets were soft and so much more inviting than the prison cell and the wildness of the Arabian night. "I'm named after a poet," he added.

Shaharazad was delighted. "A poet! I love poets!" She blushed. "I mean, I love poetry."

He nodded. "I know."

"And how would you have such knowledge?"

He handed back the cup. "You love poetry because you think you are Shaharazad." He stood up and held out his hand. "And we have to go."

She remained kneeling. "Go? It was my understanding that you were to tell me why the people weep. I know you found Mohassin, for the story has circulated throughout the palace. What has happened to change our plan? Do we need to go elsewhere for me to hear your answer?"

Yeats gestured for quiet and moved to the door. He listened. Still no sound. "Shari! You must come with me. My friends are risking their lives running from your palace guards. I don't know how much time we have."

The girl nodded. "You speak truly that there is little time. But why do you insist that I must go with you? I have not decided what I will do until I know the answer to my question. You were to find answers. I thought you came to tell me why the people weep. I thought you were sent to tell me my adventure. I thought the voice and the pictures I saw . . ." Her words trailed off.

Yeats shook his head. "I don't know anything about that." It was so hard to be attentive to what she was saying while he was listening intently for the guards' return.

Frowning and looking disappointed, she stood and walked slowly to her bed, keeping her eyes on him as she went. When she turned there was a scimitar in her hands with the sharp end aimed at Yeats's head.

"Hey, put that down," he said. "I can tell you

what is happening. I can explain. You don't need to point that at me."

She moved closer, aiming the blade at his chest. "Who are you? Why would you take me from here?"

"Because this is not where you belong," he spluttered. "You're not from here. My father—"

The blade shifted to his neck. He closed his eyes for a second as the blade touched his skin. "Please don't do that," he whispered. "Put it down." He stepped back slowly until his back was pressed against the door. On the carpeted floor their feet did not make a sound. The girl moved with unnerving ease.

"Who are you?" she repeated.

"I told you! I am Yeats. And I am here to help you."

"Why?"

Yeats sucked in a breath as the blade pushed a little more firmly into his flesh. Her manner was far too much like Khan's for his liking. "I tried to tell you in the garden. The problem is that it sounds so crazy. I just don't know if you will believe me. But

I really, really need you to believe me. I've come a long way to bring you home."

The girl stared without giving away her thoughts.

Desperate, Yeats tried another tack. "If I tell you why the people weep, will you come with me?"

Shaharazad took a step backward yet with her sword still raised. "Let us say that I will give more consideration to your words. I will reward you for telling me the truth. Although what that reward shall be remains in my discretion."

Yeats let his shoulders relax. He took a breath. Although he still felt a long way from accomplishing his goal, keeping her talking was better than having her chop him in half with a scimitar. But the risk! Once she found out about the weeping she might never want to come home.

"Guards will be here any moment," the girl said quietly. "Tell me the answer to my question. Why do the people weep?"

Yeats thought of Mr. Sutcliff. All these years he had tried to bring his granddaughter home, and now Yeats was faced with answering a question that might seal the girl's fate forever in the book. And yet, he reasoned, it was Mr. Sutcliff, after all, who said, *We cannot claim to have lived life unless we have taken risks.* He took strength from the old man's words and faced the girl again. "The people are weeping because the king of this land is murdering all the young maidens," he said firmly.

Her eyes widened. Her mouth dropped open.

Yeats continued. "His first wife betrayed him and he is determined to never trust a woman again. He marries a new girl each day and then . . ."

Shaharazad lowered her sword. Her face was ashen. "The king is killing the young women," she repeated, stunned. "How many?"

Yeats thought of the wall of white stones he had seen in the town. "I think hundreds."

Shaharazad squeezed her eyes shut. "And I have not been told."

"For your own safety. The king has allowed you to live because you are his vizier's daughter. At least, that is how I heard it."

She nodded slowly.

Yeats rushed forward and took the scimitar. She did not resist. Instead, she threw herself on the bed, burying her face in the pillows. Yeats stood awkwardly, staring from the sword to the girl. When she did not calm down quickly, he dropped the scimitar on the carpet and sat on the edge of the bed. A silk streamer hung from the canopy and tickled his nose. He blew it off.

"I'm sorry," he murmured. "I'm sure this must be very difficult for you." For a brief moment he was tempted to stroke her beautiful hair. Then he remembered his task. "Shari! Please! We have got to go. You must come with me!"

Her sobbing eased. "Why?" Her voice was muffled by the pillows. "So that I can leave my suffering people? To make certain I do not meet the fate of all the girls my age?"

Yeats punched the bedspread. He was so close.

"There are reasons I can't explain. Because you won't believe me."

"Why would I not believe you?" she said quietly.

Yeats forced himself to take a slow breath. "Do

you believe that it is possible to have too much of a good thing?" he asked.

The girl thought. "I suppose. If the good thing could be corrupted."

Nodding, Yeats answered, "Even reading and books?"

She shook her head. "How could there ever be too much of that?"

He opened his hands like a book. "What if you liked a character or story so much that you imagined yourself inside the book?"

"I have done this many times," she said.

"Yes! And you are still in a book. You have never left."

Shaharazad turned her face up to him, scowling. "How can you speak such foolishness?"

"It's not foolishness! It's the truth. You are *in a story*."

She swung away from the pillows to grip the scruff of his tunic fiercely. "Maidens are dying! And you speak like you have had too much wine!"

He gripped her wrist. "Look at me! Shari Sutcliff, look at my eyes! Do you see lies? Do I look drunk?"

The girl focused. She looked at him deeply. "No," she whispered. She touched his face. "Why do I know you?"

"Because you know my father." She slumped and he held her up. "Shari. We have to go. Now!"

The girl had gone strangely silent. Her tears ceased. Gradually she leaned away from him with a look of fixed determination.

Yeats did not let go. "Oh no! No, no, no. You can't do that."

Her eyes shifted. "Do what?"

"You can't marry the king to change his ways. Your grandfather already told me that. We have to get you out of the story now."

She blinked.

"There!" he exclaimed. "I was right. I can tell by your face. It's exactly the plan going through your mind."

Shaharazad turned away. "How did you know?"

"Like I said, you wouldn't believe me."

"You are the strangest boy I have ever met. You tell me what no one else would dare to say and then you read my mind." She threw a silk pillow across the room. "But what of it? Can you save my people? Can you stop their grief? Who will do it if not me?"

"You are not the vizier's daughter."

She wiped at a tear. "So you say."

"You are not Shaharazad." Could he pull her out the door?

Their eyes met and this time she read his thoughts. Yeats pushed off the bed. They both ran for the entrance. Yeats got one step ahead and threw himself down to block her. "No!" he gasped.

Shaharazad glared. "Eventually guards will come. I can wait. You, they'll hang. Although that is not my wish."

He blanched. "They've already tried and failed. You're coming home with me!"

She smirked. "You are too young to be my suitor."

"Suitor?"

She sighed. "I am impressed by your affections. You wish to marry me and have come to take me. It is very honorable and you are far more interesting than the older prospects my father has suggested. But this is rather unprecedented. And since you cannot walk out the door with me, past all the guards and through the palace gates, I do not see how you will fulfill your wish."

Yeats shouted, "You are not Shaharazad! You have been lost in this story for twenty years. You came here with my father, William Trafford! Remember? Remember the boat, the pirates, reading the unexpurgated version?"

Her mouth opened as if to speak and then closed quickly. She turned and walked back to the bed. "You are mad."

"Don't you dare call me *mad*!" He pounded his chest. "I am not crazy. My father is not crazy. And neither was my great-great-grandfather!" The moment the words were out of his mouth he realized just how crazy they sounded.

"Argh!" He threw up his hands. He would have to try a different approach. If he could get her to Mr. Sutcliff, the two of them together might convince her. *Provided Mr. Sutcliff was still alive.* Without the sword he could throw her over his shoulder. But she was almost his height, although not as heavy. It would be tough if she fought him. He needed Skin and Bones!

Shaharazad watched him thoughtfully. "I am honored that you are fond of me," she said. "I appreciate your sentiments and can even forgive your rashness—if you do not get in my way."

He shook his head. "I have to. You think you want to marry the king to save your people. You will be stuck in this book forever unless you come with me. This is my father's only chance. It's my family's only chance. And we are working off one last wish."

"Why do you keep on about your father?" she asked crossly.

Yeats grabbed a fistful of his hair in exasperation. "I may be here to get *you*, but I came because of *him*!" Pushing off from the door, he ran at her. He caught her off guard. She barely managed to roll away. Only the ornate bedspread separated them now.

"Please come here." He held out his hand across the cover.

"No!"

He jumped onto the spread. Shaharazad ran to the foot of the bed and swung free on the corner post. He raced after her as she rounded the bed again. They stared at each other, catching their breath.

Someone pounded on the door and Yeats's heart lurched.

"Ha!" Shaharazad triumphed. She also made her first mistake. The sleeve of her nightgown caught on the post and she stumbled. Yeats tackled her.

"Let go!"

"No! You're coming with me!"

The pounding on the door grew louder.

"Help!" Shaharazad screamed. She punched him.

Yeats seized her wrists, gripping hard. She stopped struggling. Tears welled up. "Ow," she whimpered.

Yeats was mortified. "Sorry. Sorry! But you punched me." He sat up. She pushed him hard in the chest and he fell backward. Kicking free, she made for the door before he could recover. A key turned in the latch.

"My lady!" called a familiar voice. Mohassin barreled into the room with two guards. Shaharazad ran to his arms.

"Arrest the traitor!" the cook commanded.

Yeats searched wildly for a window. The door slammed shut. The key turned in the lock. There was nowhere to go.

"What are you doing?" Mohassin spluttered furiously to the guards. "I told you to arrest the boy."

"If ye be planning to keep yer tongue a while longer," drawled Bones, "ye'd best keep it between yer teeth."

Skin doffed his hat to a dumbfounded Yeats. "We'll make a pirate of ye yet, boy."

"Hurry!" Bones called.

Yeats felt a wave of relief. "That's twice you've saved me. Thank you. But where is Mr. Sutcliff?"

Bones pointed. "She comes with us. We meet Sutcliff by the boat. Shake a leg, lad, the courtyard is sprouting guards."

Mohassin wagged his finger. "You will be caught! I promise you. Shame! Shame on you for risking the life of this great lady."

Skin glanced at Bones. "Can I cut off his tongue?"

"No time," answered his partner. "Tie him to the bed. Preferably with his face stuffed in a pillow." The pirate turned to Yeats. "Tie the girl's hands and feet." He squinted at her. "Gag her too. Ye'll have to convince her near the boat."

Shaharazad put up a tremendous fight. In the end, Yeats was forced to sit on her while Skin tied her feet.

"Rogues!" she yelled. "Why are you—" She was silenced by the gag.

"Always put the gag on first," Skin instructed Yeats.

Bones peeked into the corridor. "Guards all over the gardens! This won't be easy." For the first time, Yeats saw grim uncertainty in the pirate's face. "Fact is," Bones added, "this might be our last stand."

Shaharazad did her best to unseat Yeats.

She arched her shoulders and twisted, knocking him off balance. With her hands still untied she grabbed him. She dug her fingernails into his leg.

"Yeow!"

Shaharazad reached for his neck and found his father's necklace. She pulled and the leather strap broke. Two objects rolled onto the carpeted floor, inches from the girl's nose. The silver bell gave a final tinkle before it stopped rolling.

21

THE
NECKLACE

Shaharazad reached for the bell. Skin made to stop her, but Yeats called, "No! Let her see it."

The girl lifted the bell and turned it, listening intently to the jingle. Her gaze fell on Yeats, eyes troubled. He removed the gag from her mouth.

Skin stepped away and said, "I've seen that look before!"

Shari's gaze shifted from Yeats to Mohassin, trussed and immobile on the bed. Then she turned her attention to the Persian carpet beneath her and ran her palm along the decorated patterns. She put the bell to her ear again. Confusion filled her face. But it was a different sort of expression than when she had questioned Yeats earlier. This was something deeper, so deep that she could not manage to find her way out of it on her own. She gasped.

Yeats sat up in a hurry and offered his hand. She took it and startled him by bringing her face so close to his own that their noses touched.

"William?" she whispered. He could feel the fear and uncertainty in her grasp. But he could not stop a smile from spreading across his face. The truth was dawning!

"I'm his son. My name is Yeats. And you are Shari."

Her brows knitted.

"Not Shaharazad?"

"No. You are Shari." He put his hands on her shoulders. "I can't even imagine what you are feeling right now. But I can tell you that my father, William, was terribly confused as well. He still is, and always will be unless we get you home."

Her hands shook. "I don't know what to think."

Yeats nodded. He forced himself to speak slowly, purposefully. "Will you trust me? It is dangerous for us here."

She studied his face. "You're not William. Although I can see him in you. Your eyes! How is that?"

Still keeping his voice controlled and very aware of the pirates' impatient tapping swords, Yeats said, "There is so much to tell you that it would take a week to catch you up. I wish my father were here. I'm so proud of him. He knew the necklace was important. And it was the key to everything!" He stopped and looked at the door. "Your grandfather is here too. Do you remember him?"

She stifled a cry. "Yes, I do, I do. Where is he?"

"All right, lad," Bones interrupted. "Now's the time—if ye plan on leaving."

Yeats nodded. "Come with me . . . please."

The girl shivered. "My name is Shari. Shari Sutcliff."

"Yes, it is," Yeats affirmed.

She surveyed the luxurious room. "But I have lived here for so long," she murmured.

"You have been in a story," Yeats said gently.

"And will continue to be if we don't weigh anchor!" grumbled Skin.

"Come on," Yeats said and tugged at her sleeve.

Shari nodded and then froze when she saw poor Mohassin. "Don't hurt him," she said to the pirates. "He risked his life to save me. Other than my grandfather I've never met a more noble man."

Bones shook his head. "Not a scratch." Skin fingered his knife but grumbled in agreement. "We'd best be off," Bones added.

"Must we go so quickly?" Shari said. "I feel like I've just woken up from such a sleep. I need to think."

Catching her hand, Yeats said, "Please, we've got to go. We have to find your grandfather. And my father—William—is waiting."

"I will go with you," she said. "I must see my grandfather. I trust William . . . and I trust you too."

Yeats grinned.

Then she added, "But give me one moment." She walked to the bed and leaned toward the old man. "Mohassin," she said softly. "I will go with these rogues so that no further harm is done. Be at peace! I will be quite safe. And so will the people. Shaharazad will save her people yet!" She winked at Yeats.

As Yeats made for the door, Shari held him back. "Is William really there, beyond that door?"

"No," he said. "He's at the end of the journey. If we make it."

"I'd like to see him," she added. "I feel like I'm caught between waking and sleeping and can't decide which one is real."

"That's the way of it," Bones affirmed. Then he added with chilly calm, "But ye'd better make certain ye know which ye want most."

Yeats felt a cold shiver down his back. "What did you say?"

The pirate hefted his sword. "She's got to undo her wish. It's not good enough to remember. I told ye that."

"What do you mean?" yelled Yeats. "Look at her. We did it. We rescued her."

"Rats and ropes, lad! Ye call this rescued? There's no wish broken here."

"And we're not out of the palace yet," added

Skin. "We've a long way to the boat and who knows how many guards to fight."

Yeats stared, flabbergasted. "We might be stuck?"

Bones stamped his foot. "The deal was to rescue ye both. If one of ye chooses not to go home, then both of ye stay behind."

"What does he mean?" Shari asked quietly.

Yeats turned away. "It means we may be marooned. And my family is on the other side not knowing anything that's happened. Not only will they have lost you, they'll lose me too."

He regretted his words immediately. For Shari put her hands to her head. "My parents . . . an accident! They are gone." Her face paled.

"Easy now." Skin perked up. "Let's not bring foul weather before the sun's gone! Let's try one thing at a time." Then to Yeats, he added, "If we can win our way to the boat, ye'll have yer moment to convince the lass."

"Convince me of what?" asked Shari.

Yeats ran his fingers through his hair. He was trying to be so careful, so gentle with her, but now could not disguise his disappointment. "I guess it's not enough that you trust me," he said. "You've got to choose to come with me. With all your heart. I was so excited that you remembered that I forgot what it takes to get us back."

She studied him thoughtfully, her eyes a little more clear than a few moments before. "I'll try! But you've no idea what it feels like to be part of two places at once. Of course I want to go with you. It's an adventure. But when I look around I see everything I've ever known. And your news about the people here . . . Oh my poor people!" She brought her hands to her mouth. Then she looked at Yeats and said, "William!" She burst into tears. Confusion filled her face again. "What is happening to me?" she cried.

Yeats cast a glance helplessly at the pirates, but they would not meet his eyes. "It's not your fault," he said to Shari. "Let's get to the boat. I'll think of something!" He picked up the scimitar and turned it experimentally in his hand.

"Do you know how to use that?" Shari asked, snuffling.

Yeats swiped the air experimentally with the blade. "Not yet."

"You'd better give it to me," she said. She gazed over the room one last time, slowly, as if memorizing every carpet, every tassel, every candlestick. Then abruptly she turned and pulled Yeats to the door.

22

A
DANGEROUS RACE

The crunch of marching feet reverberated through the stone corridor. Shoulder to shoulder Yeats and Shari peered out. Moments before, Bones had extinguished the oil lamps, leaving them in semidarkness. Smoke from Shari's diversion fire still hung in the air. Despite the absence of Khan, the garden felt hostile. The ocean breeze made the branches lurch and imaginary guards lunged from every shadow.

"They've reached the near lawn now," Shari whispered in his ear. "Tell Skin to veer to the left and find the trees." After he delivered her message he felt her shiver through their clasped hands.

"It's so strange to be stealing away," she said,

ducking behind a bush. "I've spent many a night in these gardens. It was the only place I could be alone without Rawiya."

"Quiet!" snapped Skin.

Shari swung around to face the pirate. "And I'm not used to being spoken to in such a manner."

The pirate snarled and said, "Get used to it."

Yeats caught her slap in midswing. "He's a pirate, Shari!" he whispered vehemently. "He says very rude things all the time. And remember, you're not royalty."

The girl's eyes flamed. "I am here."

"He's very good with a sword," Yeats added quickly. "And probably our best chance of getting to your grandfather and my father."

Seconds later, Bones started forward. They slipped as four shadows across the lawn. Torches bobbed ahead and they could hear the jingle of armor and weapons. Behind them, they heard the sound of thudding and wood splintering as the guards launched an attack against Shaharazad's door. Mohassin would soon be free.

Skin waited for the guards to pass, then bolted

for the cover of the trees. Still hand in hand, Yeats and Shari hurried after him.

Someone shouted.

"They've seen us!" Yeats said.

"Hush up! We're nearly at the gate!" Bones answered from behind.

Shari gave a little squeal. "Gran. Is Gran all right? I haven't thought of her in oh so long!" She shook the little bell.

Bones waved frantically. "Keep her quiet!"

"Please, Shari!" Yeats implored. "You've got to stop talking. I'm sure you're remembering everything . . . and it's wonderful and all, but this is hardly the time and place. They'll kill us if we're caught. At least, they'll kill me."

She sobered instantly. "They will not! I'll have their houses turned into rubble if they try such a thing!"

"No, ye won't!" Skin whispered furiously. "Yer Mr. Sutcliff's granddaughter. The moment ye picked up that bell and remembered ye changed. Now those gents out there"—he indicated to the garden—"they may or may not believe yer the real Shaharazad. I'd rather not take the chance to find out."

Yeats squeezed her hand encouragingly. "When we get you home everything will seem right again," he said.

Shari said uncertainly, "I'm not sure where home is."

"Quiet!" Bones hissed.

They were hunkered in the same little woods in which Khan had tracked down Yeats. How long ago it felt! The gate to the beach was in sight. Guards were everywhere, thrashing the bushes with their spears and stabbing behind trees. Some carried torches and the light spread dangerously close to their hiding place. Yeats gulped. The guards would not wait to hang him this time.

"There's the gate!" Bones whispered. His sword glinted dully. "The scalawags behind us will take no prisoners, save perhaps the girl. Keep that in mind if yer legs are tired. Now, run for it!"

Something whistled through the bushes and stuck in a trunk near their heads. Skin touched the arrow embedded in the splintered bark. "Pieces of eight!" he muttered. "Half an inch from Davy Jones's locker." Yeats swallowed hard. He had an answer to his earlier question. Anyone can die in a story—even bookends.

"Through the gate!" Bones interrupted his thoughts with a shout. There was no need for silence now. Their pursuers had found them. Yeats pulled Shari along and fled after the pirates, down the darkened slope toward the water. As they ran Shari suddenly faltered.

"What is it?" asked Yeats, worried that she had been hit by an arrow.

"I can't see," she gasped.

"What do you mean?"

"I can't see anything."

"Skin and Bones!" Yeats hollered, and wrapped his arm around the girl's waist. They stumbled to the waiting pirates.

"Plagues of scurvy! What is it now?"

"It's Shari. She can't see!" Without a word Bones leaned forward, hoisted Shari over his shoulder, and whirled around again for the beach.

"Put me down, you buccaneer!" Shari said. "I can run."

"Sorry, missy. No time."

"Yeats!" Shari pleaded.

"Why can't she see?" Yeats puffed beside Skin.

"Story blindness," he said gruffly. "Seen it before. Very rare. The story's breaking down for her. It all starts to blur and fade, like empty end pages of a book. It's bad news for ye. Means she hasn't broken her wish. Ye better pray for a miracle."

"Will she be all right?"

"Does it matter?" came the reply. "We're likely all dead anyway if Sutcliff doesn't have the boat ready."

The moon lit the beach like a ghostly sunset. The salt breeze swept away the pungent aroma of the garden. Wisps of mist curled along the surface of the water. In a glimmer of moonlight Yeats spotted the figure of a man standing on the beach.

"Mr. Sutcliff!"

"Quickly, my boy!"

Mr. Sutcliff loomed over them. Bones set the

girl back on her feet. There was an intake of breath.

"Shari!"

"Grandpa!"

The girl embraced the old man. "I can't believe it's you," she said.

"It is indeed, dearest!"

"I only wish my parents were here too," she said. "I thought that perhaps, somehow, they might . . ."

"My dear," said Mr. Sutcliff, "I cannot express the overflow of my heart at this moment—"

"Good!" interrupted Bones. "'Cause yer heart will be overflowing with something else once those arrows find their mark!"

Rocks clattered behind him and Yeats spun around. Something whizzed overhead.

"Oars out, Sutcliff!" Skin hollered. "Anchors away!"

"Wait till we're afloat. Then all get in the boat," Bones shouted.

"To me, Yeats!" Mr. Sutcliff handed out orders. "Untie that rope! Here now, take hold of the other side."

Yeats hurriedly grabbed the side of the small craft. The pirates took the other side. The bottom scraped along stones. It was dreadfully heavy.

"Heave ho, lad!" Mr. Sutcliff threw in the tie rope. "Angels and minstrels of grace help us if we can't all fit." With a last effort, the boat slid into the water. Mist already covered the bow and Yeats desperately hoped it would be enough to hide them from the guards on land.

Skin gave Yeats a crooked grin. "Cutlass out, my boy! If ye can think of anything witty, this may be yer last chance to say it. Sutcliff and the girl, get in!"

Yeats stared dumbly at the pirate.

"No." Shari stepped away from the boat. "I know what to do with a scimitar. And I'm seeing a little better now."

The roaring guardsmen were fewer than thirty feet away and there was no leaving shore without a fight. The arrows had ceased. The guards had finally seen Shari. They fell silent at their final approach, and at a motion from their captain, all raised their scimitars.

"Hand-to-hand combat! My favorite!" Skin smirked. "And so many! I hardly know where to start."

"Sutcliff!" Bones yelled. "Push off and get in the boat. Hold her steady about forty feet out."

Shari and her grandfather shook their heads as one. "No!" the girl said emphatically. "I'm staying. Even blind, I can fight better than Yeats."

"I wouldn't say that," Yeats said angrily. But there was no time for more conversation. The soldiers were upon them at last. His teeth chattered. He gazed in horror at the imposing figures, all in black save their leader, whose white turban set him apart.

"Yeats!" Shari called.

"I'm right here. But I don't have a sword." The sight of Shari standing beside her grandfather with her scimitar aimed at the guards made him pause. All this way to be caught at the beach! Anger boiled inside of him. He took a deep breath and a grin began to spread. "I don't need a weapon," he said. "I'm not a killer. So let's see how many I can knock down with my fists."

Mr. Sutcliff gave Yeats an encouraging wink. "Good boy."

"Stay beside me, Yeats," said Shari.

The guards attacked like a pounding wave. Even with the pirates taking the brunt of the assault Yeats was bowled over into the sea. Someone hauled him up. Choking and spluttering, Yeats caught sight of a guard lying at his feet and rubbing his chin.

"Beginner's luck!" Bones cried. Skin had taken an opponent's weapon and was wielding a sword in each hand, singing as he fought. Shari struck expertly at the attacking soldiers, who fell back, astonished at her ferocity.

"Look out, Yeats!" Mr. Sutcliff roared.

He ducked instinctively. Someone flew over his shoulder and a knee struck his head. Reeling, he lost his footing on the sand. Everywhere, guards poured onto the beach, their torches lighting up the fight. Their little group was vastly outnumbered. It was only a matter of seconds before one of them was killed. I'm going to die! Yeats thought as he took aim at another head.

A sudden loud crack filled the air and there was a pause in the fighting. Two soldiers fell back and Yeats sank to one knee, gasping for breath.

Skin held a smoking pistol and the acrid smell of burning shot wafted over the beach. The leader of the guards grasped his shoulder, dumbfounded at the blood spreading over his tunic.

"There be more where that came from!" roared Skin. Bones dropped his cutlass and pulled two pistols from his belt.

"*Only* two more shots before he has to reload," muttered Mr. Sutcliff. "And there are many more needed to stop this tide of guardsmen, but they don't know that. It's a clever trick. I hope the guards believe it. They've likely not seen a pistol before!"

The soldiers stared at their leader in disbelief. The man fell to the ground clutching his shoulder.

"Now for it!" said Mr. Sutcliff. He hurried a protesting Shari into the shallows and they climbed into the boat. Skin caught Yeats by the back of the neck. "That's enough for ye. Fly like an albatross!" With a mighty heave Skin flung him deep into the water toward their drifting boat.

Shari gripped the bow of the boat as her grandfather swung himself on board. "Where is he, Grandpa? Where's Yeats?"

Yeats gasped from a few yards away. "Here!"

Mr. Sutcliff hauled on the oars. "Wait, my dear. Let me reel in our fish."

"Hurry, Grandpa!" Shari called.

Two more pistol shots ripped through the night air. Yeats glanced back to see the line of torches retreating, regrouping, then surging forward again. Skin and Bones had jumped into the water.

"There we are," said Mr. Sutcliff, positioning the boat as close to Yeats as possible. "Lift him under the shoulders, Shari! That's it. Easy now. Ah! Here come our pirates!"

When Yeats looked up from the bottom of the boat, Shari was hovering over him.

"Are you all right?" she asked breathlessly.

"I think so."

"You've got a cut above your eye," she said. "I expect it might hurt a bit." She touched his forehead.

"Can you see again?" he asked.

"A little. You look fuzzier than you did earlier tonight. It sort of comes and goes."

The boat suddenly dipped and they fell together to the port side. A pair of knuckles gripped the gunwale. A second later the opposite side plunged.

"For goodness' sake, are you trying to sink us?" Mr. Sutcliff shouted. The two pirates lay dripping on the bottom of the boat with Yeats and Shari squeezed in the middle.

Skin and Bones waved their arms frantically. "Row, Sutcliff, row!" The cacophony that followed, as the soldiers entered the shallows and Mr. Sutcliff started rowing, was deafening.

Skin stood. "Let me do it."

"Down, pirate!" Mr. Sutcliff roared. "You'll tip us."

"Then row like a pirate yerself," Skin retorted.

"Sit still like a good bookend," wheezed Mr. Sutcliff. It was awful for Yeats to have to lie motionless, unable to see over the side of the boat, just waiting for the guards to overtake them. His only comfort was Shari, pressed next to him.

Skin leaned up on one elbow. "Well?"

"Down," Mr. Sutcliff gasped. "Or I'll whack you with my paddle. They are aiming arrows again."

But the arrows did not reach them. The noise faded. Yeats and Shari stared up at the star-filled sky. It looked very much like the stars at home, thought Yeats.

He glanced at Shari. They were far from safe yet.

"We'll take it from here," Bones said. Mr. Sutcliff did not argue.

"That was too close," Yeats said. "I'm not much of a warrior."

Shari's smile flashed. "You were wonderful back there, Yeats! Marvelous. For someone who's never been in battle you held your ground like a hero."

He smiled weakly. "Skin said it was beginner's luck."

He wanted to tell her that she was the bravest girl he'd ever met, but she was faster. To his astonishment, she kissed his cheek. "Maybe so. But I'll think otherwise."

He looked at her hopefully.

"It's strange," Shari murmured. "I'm leaving my home that is not my home. I have memories of every part of that palace." She brought her gaze back to Yeats. "And they are not real."

Yeats raised his eyebrows. "Shari, you've been gone for twenty years. No wonder you are confused."

"Twenty years!" she groaned. She fell silent and Yeats wondered what on earth he could possibly say to make her want to go home. The slap of water against the boat's sides was soothing and both of them fell silent. Mr. Sutcliff watched them intently. The pirates, Yeats noted, kept a close eye on Mr. Sutcliff. There was a tension in the air as thick as the fear they had on the beach when facing the soldiers. Everyone was waiting. Everyone was waiting for Shari.

"I had to make a decision back there," the girl said suddenly.

"What's that?" Yeats perked up.

"When I heard the bell and saw your face—so much like William's—it took me back to Gran's house, to my old life." She looked at Yeats. "It took me back to my own story." She held the bell to her ear and smiled, remembering. "Dear William. I left him in such a terrible state, you know. The guards came from nowhere and called me Shaharazad. They bowed low and treated me like royalty. I guess I didn't have to believe it," she said. "Poor William. He tried to warn me. But I wouldn't listen. I wanted to get away from everything that reminded me of my parents."

Yeats nodded. "I can understand that. I've felt that way a bit myself recently."

"My parents are still gone." She closed her eyes for the briefest moment. "I remember now. When I'm in the story I didn't . . . I don't have to remember."

A bead of sweat or water, Yeats couldn't tell which, dropped from the end of Mr. Sutcliff's nose. The pirates were becoming restless.

"Time to go," Skin muttered. "She's not coming." At Skin's words, Yeats felt his heart thumping. They were rapidly running out of time. If Shari didn't break her wish soon the pirates would return alone. Mr. Sutcliff lowered his head and his shoulders sagged. He appeared old again. His eyes looked at Yeats pleadingly.

Yeats desperately cast about in his mind for something clever to say. He saw the bell and stifled a gasp. Reaching over, he opened her hand. He picked up the bell and in the face of the moon he held it up.

"I know why you need to wish for home," he said.

The girl sat up. "Why?"

He held her gaze steadily. Then he took the bell and put it back in her hand. He wrapped her fingers around it. "Because you were born to rescue people. It's in your name. And it's the reason you wanted to come here, to be the rescuer. But now, the people who need you most are on the other side of this story. And you are the only one who can bring us back and make a happy ending."

Shari frowned, but she was listening closely.

He pressed on. "My dad was messed up when you didn't return. My mom is ready to leave him because of it. Gran has faithfully dusted your picture and hoped for a miracle. Your grandfather risked everything to come here. He's tried for twenty years to save you. Now look at him." Yeats put his hand on her shoulder. "Shaharazad, your people need you. And they are waiting for you right now. Not outside a palace in a time from long ago. But now, at Gran's house, waiting, hoping beyond hope that you will come home."

Tears welled up in her eyes. She gave a weak smile. "You sound so much like William and yet not like William too." She sniffed and pressed the bell to her cheek. "You are right, Yeats. This isn't my story, no matter how much I feel that it is."

Bones stopped rowing and stared at her.

Shari looked at Mr. Sutcliff. "Grandpa."

"My dear," he said.

She turned to Yeats and murmured, "I think I want to go home." As her last word echoed over the water, the wind suddenly gusted and Yeats heard again a boy's voice calling, "I wish! I wish!"

The pirates heard it, too, for they sat up straight.

"That came from the well," said Skin. "I thought it was broken."

"'Tis," said Bones. "It rattled and roared for twenty years while I was marooned in the garden."

"Wait!" Yeats cried excitedly. "I've heard that voice. At the well. I threw a coin in and the whole thing erupted. That voice was calling from the well."

Shari stared keenly at him. "That was William."

"'Twas an old wish, no doubt," said Bones. "Likely yer father's, finally making its way out. Not much strength to it." Then he added with a wink, "Must have helped, though. Look to the girl!"

Shari's eyes were bright and hopeful, all doubt gone from her face. She looked at the pirates, then straight at Yeats. "I want to go home!" she said with conviction. Then, at the top of her voice, she shouted, "I want to go home!"

"Thar she blows!" roared Bones. "The old wish is broken."

Yeats leaned forward and gave Shari a bear hug. Over her shoulder, he looked at the pirates. "Can we really go home?"

"Ye can indeed," said Bones.

Skin leaned down to Yeats. "Well done, ye little

pirate," he said. "It took a mite more than just wit to win the day."

All at once, something pounced. A furry face peered up from Yeats's ankles.

"Odysseus!"

Shari scooped the cat into her arms. "Dear, dear Odysseus." Odysseus stared at Yeats with his cat's smile.

Seconds later Yeats felt the sensation of falling. The air around them changed and he clung to the gunwale. Shari felt it, too, for she sat up straight as an arrow. A deep sensation of sorrow welled up inside him. Tears formed in the corners of Shari's eyes. Then, just as quickly as it came, the feeling left, only to be replaced by an overwhelming sense of confidence.

They exchanged glances. "The sea of words," Yeats said. The wind gusted and blew their hair wildly.

"We're going home!" Shari shouted. She raised Odysseus's paws in the air triumphantly.

Yeats laughed with relief. *Home. Home and his parents.* "We're coming home, Mom and Dad!"

"We're coming, William!" Shari sang.

The wind suddenly reached gale force and Yeats and Shari clung to each other for dear life. Odysseus dug his claws in so deeply Shari yelped.

Mr. Sutcliff gave his granddaughter a jaunty wave.

Skin rowed with a fury. "Never thought I'd miss it!" he yelled above the wind.

"A wind to take us home." Mr. Sutcliff watched his granddaughter and wiped the tears from his eyes.

23

THE LIBRARY

After a thoroughly wretched afternoon Faith decided that nothing worse could happen and that perhaps it was time to call the police. "William?"

Her husband closed the book with a snap. He put a finger to his lips. "Shhh."

"What is it?" Gran whispered and set down the tea.

William looked at Gran. "Someone just called my name." He tapped the book. "From inside."

"Well, for heaven's sake, don't close it!" Faith stepped toward him.

He shook his head, his eyes widening. "It doesn't matter. I think . . . I think . . . they are—"

A wind tore through the library. Loose pages flew wildly above their heads and pages flapped in chorus from every shelf in the room. Several seconds later, three people and one cat appeared on the floor.

After a breathless moment of silence, Faith cried and pounced on the figure nearest to her. "Yeats!"

William froze, his eyes moving from his son to the person sitting next to him. Faith stopped fussing over the cut above Yeats's eye as the new arrivals slowly rose to their feet. A page from the book fluttered to the floor.

"Hello, William," Shari said softly.

Tears flowed freely down William's cheeks.

She embraced him. Wrapping her small arms around William, she patted his back while he wept. "I'm back, finally." She pulled away to look at him. "And let me say—you are old! Do you remember how we used to imagine what we would look like when we were ancient? We used to put our hands out and pretend they were wrinkled."

William couldn't speak. Yeats walked to his father and threw his arm around his shoulders.

"Thank you, son," William gasped.

Yeats looked him square in the eye. "Thank *you*, Dad. You gave me the necklace. You knew it was important. It was! We were stuck there. I couldn't get Shari to remember. When she saw the bell she remembered everything."

His father nodded. "My heart told me you needed it. Thank God, for once I was right."

"And your wishes at the well! One of them made it through. I put a coin in and one of them got out. It helped Shari choose to come home. You've been right all your life, Dad." Yeats grinned. "There is no madness in our family. It was just so hard for everyone else to believe."

Faith wiped her eyes. "Especially me."

William looked up hopefully.

Shari sighed. "I kind of like this. You've gotten old." She shifted her gaze to Yeats. "But I get to stay a kid!"

"For the moment," said Mr. Sutcliff thoughtfully. "I do believe, however, that all will progress normally now." He grinned. "As normal as childhood can be. For there seems to be enough magic in it to last a lifetime."

William wiped his eyes. "You haven't changed at all," he said to Shari. "I feel like there's a part of me that's still twelve. Like I've gone back. But I know I can't. Shari, this is Faith. She is—"

"I'm his wife." Faith stood beside her husband and took his hand. Yeats hugged them both.

"I knew William would marry someone pretty," said Shari.

"Welcome home," Faith said. "And thank you."

Shari nodded. "In the palace, you would have all the young men running after you. . . ." She paused, suddenly troubled, as if stirred by a memory.

"I fear," said her grandfather, "that you will find the memory of your adventure lingering for many a year to come."

Shari ran to him.

Gran moved over to them and ran her hands through the girl's hair. "Exactly the same as when you left." She stifled a sob.

Odysseus growled at the shelf. The bookends were back in place.

Yeats pointed. "Skin and Bones!"

The metal pirates remained frozen.

Mr. Sutcliff smiled. "Hats off to you gentle-men." He glanced at the ceiling and lowered his voice. "For pirates, I've never known any so gallant."

"How about some tea?" Gran asked and gestured to the kitchen. "I think we've all had enough adventures to fill twenty years."

"To quote a favorite of mine"—Mr. Sutcliff put his hand over his heart—"'All's well that ends well!'"

24

A BEGINNING
OF ENDS

Yeats could not sleep. He lay against the pillows and stared at the ceiling. For all the happiness of seeing his parents restored and spending time with Shari, he somehow could not quiet a pang of ill ease. The bed creaked as he sat up.

Roland. In the wildness of their escape and the joy of his family's reconciliation he had forgotten about his friend. He thought of Khan and hoped the great cat had made a successful rescue. In all likelihood his friend was free. But what if Roland was still there? What if Khan couldn't get him out? The stark shadow of the gallows tree made him shiver.

There was a noise in the passage outside. A second later the door squeaked open and in the dim light of the hall stood Shari, dressed in one of Gran's nightgowns.

"Hello," she whispered. "You awake?"

"Yeah."

"Can I come in?"

"Sure."

A few steps farther and she stopped. She glanced at the long gown. "Not exactly royal, is it?"

Yeats raised his eyebrows. "That's not what I was thinking. You could wear anything and you'd be pretty."

She smiled. "Son of a poet." She plunked herself down on the end of his bed. "I can't sleep. I don't think I will for days and days. There's far too much to think about, even after all that talking to William . . . your father."

Yeats nodded. "Every once in a while I start shaking."

"It was so exciting!"

"It was, wasn't it?" he said.

She frowned. "Although, so painful to see

everyone old. It's not something you want to experience, trust me."

He regarded her thoughtfully. "And I can't stop thinking about Roland."

"Who?"

He told her about running from the guards and being put in a cell. As he described his time with his friend and fellow prisoner she nodded knowingly. "I wondered why Khan was gone so often at night. I used to think that he preferred the cool air of the garden to the warmth of my room."

"Now you know," Yeats answered.

She scowled. "I hate to think of somebody else being left behind."

The memory of his prison cell with its rigid bars and grate in the ceiling made Yeats shiver. "I hope Khan rescued him."

Shari suddenly put her hand to her mouth. "What did you say your friend's name was?"

"Roland."

"Wait here," she commanded. She leapt off the bed and disappeared out the door. A moment later she returned and held out an envelope.

"Grandpa said to give this to you. He said it came special delivery today while we were talking in the back garden."

Yeats took the envelope and turned it over. "It's from Roland!" he said incredulously. "But how . . . ?"

"Open it!" cried Shari.

Yeats tore the envelope open. "I can't believe it; I can't believe it," he murmured.

"Oh, give it to me," said Shari. She took the letter and began to read aloud. *"Yeats! It's me, Roland! I am safe and sound, thanks to you. Khan came and got me and took me right home. You saved my life! I've been here a couple of days and I found your gran's address. I'm writing this quickly so it gets to you. You can reach me at the number at the bottom of the page. It's too expensive to fly to the USA and see you (and how could we explain knowing each other?), but I think I've got another way. I made a deal with Khan. Not sure if you'll be the first to read this, so . . . My wish is his command. Do you get it? I can't remember your girlfriend's name . . ."*

Shari looked up. "Your girlfriend?" Her eyes widened. "Oh! He means me."

Yeats and Shari both turned bright red and she quickly began reading again.

". . . *but if you two would like to 'meet' me, we can. Know what I mean? Contact me no matter what! I will always be your friend, Roland.*"

Shari said, "That's all."

"I can't believe it!" Yeats said again. "It's too good to be true."

"I'd like to meet him," said Shari.

"I want to see him again," said Yeats. "It would be so strange. I mean, the last time we saw each other we were in prison!"

They were both quiet for a moment. Then Shari said, "How did the letter get here so quickly? We only got back today."

Yeats was thinking hard. "Your grandfather said something to me about that. He said that time in the story world was different from ours. He found that out when he entered the story. I'd only been gone an hour here and yet he found me in a prison—hours and hours later. And it must be. I mean, look at you. You should be twenty years older. And then, of course, there's Odysseus."

Shari nodded. "So Roland must have beat us back and had time to write a letter!"

"But what does he mean by 'meet' him?" asked Yeats.

The quiet patter of paws made them both turn. "Odysseus, dear." Shari scooped him up and placed the cat in between them. He circled them, kneading the bedspread and purring.

Yeats looked up at Shari. "That's another thing."

"What?"

"Odysseus can grow old now. The pirates told me he couldn't die until you returned."

"Die? How awful!"

"He's got to go sometime."

She gave Yeats a frown. "Must you be so practical?"

He shook his head. "I don't want Odysseus to die either. And it's not as if he'll pop off tomorrow. He's a young cat. It's just that his clock has started again."

They fell silent listening to the wind whine around the old house and rattle the shutters.

Shari kept staring at him with her eyes half shut. "Of course!" she said presently.

"What?"

"I think I know what Roland is up to. And I know who can help us."

"Who?"

The girl's smile grew wide. "Come with me!" She reached for his hand.

On the first step of the staircase the boards screeched out a protest. Shari burst into giggles. "I keep forgetting!"

"Shhh!" Yeats whispered vehemently. His parents were exhausted, and he didn't want to alarm them.

"Where are we going?" asked Yeats suspiciously.

"The library."

Yeats stopped short. "No. We can't go there. Not after everything we've been through."

"We're not going to do anything. We're just going to ask a question." She plucked at his shirt. "Come on, brave Yeats."

They stole through the kitchen and followed

the hallway down to the infamous doors. Yeats stopped.

"No! This isn't right!"

"It's just a question."

"To who?"

Shari pushed the door and stepped inside.

Exasperated, Yeats waited for several seconds before entering. Shari was bathed in moonlight, frozen below the ticking clock, staring. Yeats followed her gaze to the bronze pirates now guarding a full shelf of books.

"Shari!" he growled, surprised at the force in his own voice. He stepped to her side.

She knelt in front of the bookends. Despite his anger Yeats couldn't stop his curiosity. He leaned down for a peek.

Shari gave a little wave. "Hello, boys!" She glanced at Yeats but all was quiet. "Skin? Bones? We have a very important question for you." Yeats crouched beside her, half expecting to hear a gruff, piratey voice responding. But the pirates remained frozen.

Yeats looked for the peg leg. "You're talking to Skin."

"It doesn't look as if anything ever happened, does it?" she murmured.

Yeats turned to her. "Yeah, but we know better."

She tapped the spine of a small book. "We certainly do." She gave Yeats a mischievous smile. Then she cupped her hands to his ear and whispered, "I think we have more wishes."

Yeats pulled back to say, "We've used it up. Both of us."

She put her mouth back to his ear. "There are two pirates. You caught Skin talking and I did too. That leaves one pirate and two wishes between us!"

"The scalawags!" hissed Yeats. "They never . . ."

Shari covered his mouth with her hand. "And we won't mention it either, will we?"

He nodded and fell silent. Then he said, "I did think that we might try the wishing well. But it was so badly broken. I think my father's wish was the last one to make it out."

"We'll make our plans upstairs and out of earshot," she said. She traced her finger across the spines of the books between the pirates. Then she whispered, "It would be fun to use our wish in one of these, wouldn't it?" Her large brown eyes turned to him. "It wouldn't matter which book we started with as long as we could meet Roland." She made a motion with her finger and pointed at Collfield's unexpurgated version.

Yeats shivered. "Don't even think it!"

"Do you want to see Roland?"

"Yes! But—"

She shrugged. "Well, then." She slid out the small volume she had touched earlier. "I think we can make our wish and then enter any story and we'll be able to meet him. We just have to agree when and where. Wouldn't it be fun?"

They stared at each other for long time.

"Not sure I can make a choice like that so quickly," said Yeats.

"We don't have to decide tonight," she replied.

His thoughts drifted to his parents, sleeping

so peacefully upstairs, and to Mr. Sutcliff, whose long wait had finally been rewarded.

He took the book from Shari's hand. "What story is it anyway?" he asked gruffly. He turned it over.

Treasure Island.

ABOUT THE AUTHOR

David Ward was born in Montreal and grew up in Vancouver. He is the author of the Grassland Trilogy and is a university instructor in children's literature. He lives in Portland, Oregon, with his wife and three children.

This book was designed by Melissa Arnst and art directed by Chad W. Beckerman. The text is set in 12-point Baskerville, a font designed in 1757 by John Baskerville, an English typographer and printer. Somewhat dissatisfied with the heavy popular type styles of the time, he created his own distinct style, which was more delicate. He examined various faces for their ease of reading, and found that finer types were easier to read when printed in the smaller sizes used in books. Baskerville's type style is appreciated today as one of the best type choices for printed books. The display font used is Sackers Solid Antique.